"A moving and memorable tale . . . taut, spare, and nobly wrought.

"[It] stretches from Vermont to China to link the loyalties and longings, the joys and sufferings that constitute the endless variety and the unchanging sameness of the family of man."

—*The New York Times*

"Pearl Buck in top form."

—*Pittsburgh Press*

"A gripping story."

—*St. Louis Globe-Democrat*

"Deeply moving . . . mounting suspense."

—*Philadelphia Bulletin*

"The towering woman author of our time."

—*The Ladies' Home Journal*

LETTER . . . was original . . . The John Day Company, Inc.

## Books by Pearl S. Buck

Published by POCKET BOOKS

# Pearl S. BUCK

## Letter from Peking

A POCKET BOOK EDITION published by
Simon & Schuster of Canada, Ltd. • Markham, Ontario, Canada
Registered User of the Trademark

LETTER FROM PEKING

John Day edition published 1957

POCKET BOOK edition published November, 1958
7th printing.........August, 1975

Standard Book Number: 671-80111-2.

Front cover illustration by James Avati.

Printed in Canada.

"In the arts everything that is beautiful pleases me. I know no exclusivity. I do not believe in any one school. I like what is gay as well as what is serious, the terrible, the great, the small. In short, everything which is as it ought to be: truthful and beautiful."

—Verdi to the painter Morelli

# Letter from Peking

THE YEAR IS 1950, the month is September, and the day the twenty-fifth. The place? It is this valley in the mountains of Vermont, where I was born and where I lived my childhood through. I have crossed the seas, I made my love's country my own. Then came war, and I was an alien in spite of love, and I returned again to the valley.

Half an hour ago I walked down our country road, under the arch of maples, red and gold, to meet the postman. He comes only three times a week to this remote spot in the mountains of Vermont, and three mornings a week I wake early and restless. There is always the chance that a letter will come from Peking, a letter from Gerald. For months no letter has come. But this morning there was a letter. The postman singled it out and gave it to me.

"Here's what you're waitin' for," he said.

I would not open it until he was gone. Then, alone in the lane, under the arching maple trees blazing with autumn fire, I opened the envelope. I knew, as

1

I read, that I had been expecting this letter. No, rather, I knew that it could not surprise me. Nothing that Gerald does can surprise me, or shock me, or even hurt me. I have loved him. I do love him, and shall always love him.

I read the letter, over and over again. In the silent autumn air, no wind stirring, the bright leaves floated down. I could hear Gerald's voice speaking the words he had written.

MY DEAR WIFE:

First, before I say what must be said, let me tell you that I love only you. Whatever I do now, remember that it is you I love. If you never receive a letter from me again, know that in my heart I write you every day.

These were the opening words of the letter, and as I read them I knew what must follow. I read to the end, and then, Gerald's voice echoing in my ears, I walked home. The house is empty after Rennie leaves for school. I am glad for this loneliness. I am here now in my room, at my desk, writing. I have locked the letter into my box. I will forget it. At least for a while let me forget, until the numbness has gone from my heart. This is my comfort, to write down all I feel, since there is no one to whom I can speak.

Yet this morning dawned like any other day. I rise early nowadays. Our neighbor farmers rise at four and sleep soon after twilight, as Chinese farmers do. But Gerald likes the quiet while others sleep, and so, through the years of our marriage, I have learned to go late to bed. The night hours in our small Chinese house were sweet. The street sounds died after dark, and if there was music, it came when the day's business was finished. Over the low compound walls the voice of a two-stringed violin floated into our courts. It was made by our neighbor, Mr. Hua, who by day was a merchant in a nearby silk shop. In summer Gerald and I sat under the pine tree by the goldfish pool, and we let Rennie, our son, stay with us past all sensible bedtime for a child. He is our only son. Our daughter died suddenly in babyhood. In the morning she was laughing and alive, and by night she was gone. I do not know why she died. The sorrow was part of the price I paid for loving Gerald and going with him to China.

For a long time, it seemed very long, we were childless. I grieved but I was saved by Gerald's grief. I thought he would never cease mourning for our lost child. For months he could not sleep easily and he ate so little that his tall frame, always slender, was skeleton. I suppressed my own tears to listen to his grieving.

"I should have stayed in your country," he said again and again. "If we had lived in America, our daughter would not have died. I have robbed you of too much."

I leaned my head upon his breast. "Wherever you go, there I go. There is no cost in comparison."

He looked at me strangely. "This is the difference between American women and Chinese women. You are more wife than mother."

"When I am with you I am all wife," I said. "And besides, you would never have been happy in America."

He could not be happy here. I knew it then and I know it now. Though in Peking I was often homesick in fleeting moments for the clean cool mountains of

Vermont, I was happy there. It is a jewel of a city, richly set, gilded with time and history, the people courteous and gay, and I saw my life stretching ahead of me in peace and beauty, and there, I supposed, I would be buried by Gerald's side, both of us old and full of years. We come of long-lived stock, he and I.

Yet here I am, in this Vermont village of Raleigh, in a lonely farmhouse, with Rennie, our son, seventeen years old. And now, this letter having come, I do not think I shall ever see Gerald again.

. . . As I said, the day began as any other does. I rose at six, I helped Matt milk our four cows and I set the can on the barn stoop for the milk truck to pick up, saving out the big pewter pitcher full for Rennie. Then I went into the kitchen and made his breakfast. Rennie helps to milk at night. He is like Gerald. To rise early is torture but he will work late and with ease. I, being alone, have returned to the hours of my childhood, for I was born here upon this land which belonged to my grandfather and then to my father, and now is mine. By hope and faith my father was an inventor in a minor way, scamping his farm work to build "contraptions," as he called them. Two or three were fairly successful, an egg-washing machine, for example. But we fed from the farm and for cash depended upon a legacy left my father by his father, who was not a farmer but a famous lawyer. When Gerald and I were married, my father was already dead, and my mother lived here alone. She died before Rennie was born and left me the farm, and Matt Greene took care of it while I was in Peking, and he comes every day as he always has. For when we saw that we must part, Gerald and I, it was to this place that I returned. There was no other.

4

So then, Rennie came down this morning, his cheeks rosy from the cold night air of windows open in his bedroom. "Good morning, Mother," he said, and kissed my cheek.

"Good morning, son," I said.

This ritual his father has always insisted upon. We greet each other, when we have been apart.

"When you leave the presence of your parents," Gerald instructed his son, "then you must say good-bye to them, you must tell them where you go, and immediately upon your return you must show yourself before them and inquire how they are. This is filial piety."

"How are you this morning, Mother?" Rennie inquired.

"Very well, thank you," I said.

"I hope you slept?"

"I did, thank you," I said.

We smiled at each other, Rennie and I, remembering Gerald, he his father, I, my husband. Rennie looks like his father. He is tall for his age. Hair and eyes are black, and his skin, smooth as only Chinese ancestors can bequeath, is the color of Guernsey cream. His profile is beautiful, the features subtly subdued and yet strong.

"Sit down, son," I said. "Your breakfast is ready."

Breakfast for Rennie is a monumental meal. He heaps his oatmeal with brown sugar and rich milk. Gerald has forbidden white sugar, and in Peking we used only the dark Chinese sugar. Milk is American, but Rennie is American too, his Chinese blood only one-fourth of his ancestral inheritance. His body is not Chinese. He is strong-boned, his hands and feet are well shaped but big, and he has not his father's elegant structure.

"Three eggs, please," he said as usual.

It is a good thing I have hens. My small legacy would not suffice for eggs and meat on the scale that Rennie enjoys. Bacon, too, is a luxury, but I delight to provide it for my son. . . . I must not so soon begin to say mine, instead of ours. Rennie is also Gerald's son. Let me not forget. But I do not know how much the letter will change my life.

The dining-room window looks on the road, conveniently, and from his seat at the head of the table, Rennie can see the school bus coming. At first we left the seat empty, against the time when husband and father might sit there. For when we left Gerald on the wharf at Shanghai, he said he might join us in three months. At the end of three months he said nothing of his coming, and his letters were already weeks apart. So, because he could see the road, Rennie said he would take his father's chair for the present, and I did not say yes or no. Perhaps I knew already that the letter was on its way.

"There's the bus," Rennie shouted. His eggs and bacon were gone, so were three slices of brown toast and butter, and he drank down his second glass of milk and reached for his windbreaker and cap.

"Good-bye, Mother!"

"Good-bye, son," I said.

Gerald has never allowed an abbreviation of my name. When Rennie learned from American children in Shanghai to say Mom or Ma, Gerald was stern.

"Mother is a beautiful word," he said gravely. "You shall not corrupt it."

He spoke in Chinese as he always does when he wishes to teach his son, and Rennie obeyed.

When I was alone, the house silent about me, I did my usual work. I washed the dishes and then went upstairs to make the beds. My room, the one my parents used, stretches across the front of the house. It has five windows and the landscape changes with every day and hour. This morning when I rose at six the golden moon, round and huge, was sinking behind the wooded mountains. The level rays were still strong enough to make black shadows from the pointed cedars upon the gray rocks beneath. I loved the safety of our compound walls in Peking, but I love this landscape better. Without Gerald, I choose my own country. With him any land serves and all are beautiful.

Facing south, my room on a fair day is lit with sunshine. I made the big four-poster bed and dusted the bureaus and chests and the white-painted chimney piece. The air is dustless and the floor needs only a brief polishing. I wonder sometimes that I labor so easily here in this house, when in our Chinese house I needed five servants, or thought I did. Gerald said I did. He did not like to see me work with my hands. It is true that I have nice hands. It was the first thing he said to me.

"You have lovely hands."

I held them up to look at.

"Do I?" I asked stupidly. No, not stupidly, for I wanted to hear him say it again.

"American girls do not usually have good hands," he went on. "I notice this because my mother, being Chinese, had exquisite hands."

"Do all Chinese women have exquisite hands?" I asked.

7

"Yes."

I think he never spoke of my hands again, but I have not forgotten. Perhaps he began to love me because my hands made him think of his mother's. How can I know now?

It has been nearly three months since I have had a letter from Gerald—until today. The letter is mailed not from Shanghai but from Hongkong, and it is inside an envelope addressed by a strange hand.

"You must not worry if my letters are far apart now," Gerald writes. "I cannot tell you the difficulties," he writes. "I cannot even tell you how this letter reaches you. When you answer, do not send the letter to me, but to the address on the envelope. It may be months before I can reply."

We used, at first, to write every day when we were apart. But until the war with Japan came, we were never apart. Then, when it seemed that the northern provinces would fall easily to the enemy, Gerald said I must take Rennie to Chungking before the railroad to Hankow was cut.

"Without you?" I cried.

"I will follow when I can," he said. "I cannot leave until the college leaves with me."

He was the president of the university, and responsibility was heavy upon him. I knew he was right, and Rennie and I set forth alone for Chungking. It was not an easy journey. The train was crowded with refugees, who clung even upon the roofs of the cars, and the hotel in Hankow was full of the escaping rich and their retinues. I made the most of the dying prestige of the white man and found a tiny space for Rennie and me, and by urgency and bribes, I bought

8

a passage upon the small steamer that makes the perilous journey up the Yangtse gorges to Chungking.

Thither Gerald was to follow, and he did, months later, his students and faculty with him. Meanwhile Rennie and I had found a small house in the hills above the city. Oh, the joy of reunion with the beloved! He came in, so gaunt he seemed to have added inches to his height. But he was content. His students and faculty had stayed with him, he had led them to safety. The city gentry had given him the use of several ancient ancestral halls, and all were housed. He had seen them safe and fed before he came home to me.

When I put my arms about him that day I felt him tremble and knew how tired he was.

"Here you can rest," I told him.

He looked about the home I had made. I have a passion for big rooms. When I first found the brick farmhouse we rented near Chungking, I told the owner that I would take it only if he allowed me to tear out two partitions in the main building and make three rooms into one large room.

"Where will you sleep?" he asked, rolling his little eyes and wagging his head. He was a fat fellow, shaven-pated and dirty, an owner and not a farmer, living on his rents.

I pretended I had not heard him. It was none of his business. I had already planned to use the two storerooms on either side of the enclosed court as bedrooms. The gatehouse rooms would do for kitchen and stores. Therefore the room that Gerald saw was large and comfortable. True, we had brought nothing with us from our Peking house, but I knew how to find what

I needed in the small shops of any Chinese city. Chinese craftsmen are skilled and they love beauty.

"You have the genius of a homemaker," Gerald said. He sat down in a cushioned wicker chair and leaned his head back.

"It is heaven," he said, and closed his eyes.

I cannot write for crying—

It is already the first day of February. For weeks our Vermont landscape has been winterbound, the mountains white and the valley silent under snow. Three days ago a warm wind and sunshine melted the snow on the hillside and the roads, a deceptive thaw, I know, for winter will come back again. We have some of our deepest snows in March, and even in April. Sometimes the spring sugaring is delayed for days because the sap freezes in the pipes on its way down to the sugar house. Today the valley is hidden in mist and the mountains have vanished. I can see no further than the gate to the dooryard. My father put up the fence for my mother who, Boston reared, could not bear the frightening distances she saw from the windows of this house, the mountains rolling away.

"I must live behind a gate," she told my father, "else how do I know where I belong?"

He put up the fence, enclosing plenty of lawn and the clump of big white birch. My mother was a pretty woman, slender as long as she lived, and she lived years after my father died. But she was rigid in mind and body. She demanded fences and gates and she seldom went beyond them. When I told her I wanted to marry Gerald MacLeod she was not pleased. She had not enjoyed marriage, in spite of loving my father, and she did not want me to marry.

"There is much in marriage that is distasteful to a nice woman." This she said when I asked her why she did not want me to marry. "Although MacLeod is a good name," she added.

I considered for one moment whether I would tell her next that Gerald was half-Chinese. He can pass for a dark Caucasian, for while his eyes are slightly almond-shaped, they are large and his brows are handsome. He is far more beautiful as a man than I am as a woman. I am small and fair and my eyes are gray rather than blue. I have never been sure I was pretty. Gerald has not told me I was pretty.

"Your skin is exquisite."

"Your mouth is very sweet."

Such words he has said, defining attributes but never declaring beauty. With all my heart I declared his beauty. For indeed there is some magic in the mingling of blood. Yet from which side the magic comes, who knows? It is the formula that provides the freshness. . . .

But if I considered concealing Gerald's Chinese blood, it was only for a moment. My mother was exceedingly acute. She could surmise what she did not know. I said, carefully casual, "Gerald's father lives in Peking. He is American but he married a Chinese lady and so Gerald is half-Chinese."

My mother's little mouth opened. She looked at me with horror.

"Oh, Elizabeth—no!"

Only my mother called me Elizabeth. I am named for my grandmother, Elizabeth Duane. Gerald calls

11

me Eve. It is his love name for me. By others I am called by every possible variation.

"Eve," he said, that day when we were newly betrothed, "you are my first love."

"Shall I call you Adam?" I asked half-playfully.

He looked half-amused, half-cynical. "I doubt that Christians would concede the name to a Chinese," he remarked.

"You insist upon being Chinese, but you aren't—not by half," I retorted. "And please, Gerald, when you meet my mother, be the American half."

He became very Chinese at this, and made a show of being inscrutable and polite and evasive, all with humor, and I did not know how he would behave to my mother. I sorrowed that my father was dead, for he would have enjoyed Gerald, and might even have reveled in his being half-Chinese. The windows of my father's mind were open to the world. When he died, I kept the windows open.

Nevertheless, I should have trusted Gerald, for when he met my mother, he appeared before her as an extremely handsome young American, his Chinese ancestry escaping only in his suave and natural grace, and in the straightness of his sleekly brushed and very black hair. Even his eyes were alert and frank. Sometimes they were Chinese in their look, revealing the self-contained and sometimes distant person who lives within the soul of my beloved.

My mother could be distant too, in her small way, and on that day she was frigid. She sat in the parlor to receive him, dressed in her gray silk. Beside her was the mahogany tea table and the silver tea set her mother had left her, and the best porcelain cups and saucers which a seafaring ancestor brought home from Canton, China, a hundred years ago.

"Mother," I said, "this is Gerald."

My mother put out her small, pale hand. "How do you do," she murmured. She was a little woman but she could put on immense dignity and did so.

"I am well, thank you," Gerald said in his warm pleasant voice, "and very happy, Mrs. Kirke, to meet you."

"Sit down, Gerald," I said, trying to be at ease while I was instantly furious with my mother. For she could be amiable if she wished, never quite losing her dignity, but gentling it. She had a rare but pretty smile. There was no hint of it now on her severe narrow face.

"Such a beautiful house," Gerald said, looking about him. "I like these old houses that belong to their landscapes."

My mother was unwillingly pleased. "It's too big," she said, and began to pour tea.

"There is no need for houses to be small," Gerald said. "A house should be like a gem, always in proportion to its setting."

"I suppose you would like China tea," my mother said, "but we always use Indian."

"I would like it then with cream," Gerald said. He was composed and at ease, while, as I could see, he was quite aware of my mother's mood. And when he had his tea and was eating scones, for my mother could be very English when she chose, and she always chose to be so when she put on all her dignity, Gerald said, "Ah, scones! I haven't had these since my Scotch grandmother died."

"Oh, and was your grandmother Scotch?" my mother inquired.

"She was, although her family emigrated early to Virginia," Gerald said. "When I was small, however, she came to visit us and she liked our city so well that she stayed until she died, and we buried her in the cemetery with the other white people."

"What was your city?" my mother asked, nibbling her scone.

"Peking, the ancient capital of China," Gerald said, exactly as though he might have said London or Paris or Rome. "This is good tea," he said. "Indian tea can be quite bad, as Chinese tea can be, too. You are a connoisseur, Mrs. Kirke."

"I was taught as a girl to know my teas," my mother said. She was trying not to unbend and she made a pretense of lifting the cake plate and then put it down again.

Gerald laughed. "In a minute, please! Grandmother taught me not to take cake while I was still eating scone."

Mother had to smile then, a very small, cool smile, but I laughed, partly at her and partly because I was happy.

"You were too well brought up, Gerald," I said.

My mother instantly turned on me. "Elizabeth, I do not understand that remark. You yourself have been well brought up, I think, and Mr. MacLeod is entirely right, and you shouldn't be facetious at the wrong time."

"I'm sorry, Mother," I said. It was the slogan of my childhood, taught me in secret by my father. "Liz," he said, and Liz was his version of my stately name, "Liz, it's so easy to say 'I'm sorry.' It costs nothing and it saves a mint of pain. Those two words are the

14

common coin of daily life, but especially between people who love each other."

My mother turned her profile to me and she chose to speak to Gerald.

"Did your grandmother MacLeod live in Richmond?" she asked.

"She did," he said. "There are old Scotch families in Virginia, and my grandmother always insisted that her great-great-grandfather Daniel was among the first founders. Perhaps he was."

"Very interesting," my mother said. Family trees were her hobby and I saw that I need not exert myself. Gerald had won her cool little heart, so far as it could be won.

This is not to say that she had no misgivings. More than once after that, when Gerald came to visit before we were married, she summoned me to her room late at night, after Gerald and I had parted, and there she sat upright in her Windsor chair, wrapped in her gray flannelette dressing gown and her hair in black kid curlers.

"Elizabeth, I have a dreadful fear that when you have a child it will look Chinese. Children do take after the grandparents. You are the image of your Grandmother Duane."

"He might look like the MacLeods," I suggested.

"There's no guarantee," she retorted, "and how I could bear to have a Chinese grandchild I do not know. I could not explain it in Boston."

For my mother was never a true Vermonter but always a citizen of Boston, spiritually and mentally.

"Don't worry, Mother," I said. "Gerald and I will live in Peking."

15

This startled her indeed. "You'll never go and live in China," she said, remonstrating.

"Didn't you come and live in Vermont?" I parried.

"But China," she persisted.

"Peking is no more remote than London or Paris or Rome," I said, echoing the beloved.

"I never knew anyone to go to Peking," she said, resisting the idea of its nearness.

"Grandmother MacLeod went," I reminded her. "What's more, she's buried there."

"She couldn't help dying, wherever she was," my mother declared and grimly.

"She wanted to be buried there—Gerald says so."

My mother could only sigh.

"Kiss me good night," she said. "I'll never go to Peking," she added as I leaned to kiss her cheek.

"You might," I said gaily. I was too happy to be anything but gay in those days, though she shook her head.

She was right. She never went to Peking. Within a year after Gerald and I were married, she died of a sudden chill that developed quickly into pneumonia and I remembered what she had said every winter, drawing her gray shawl about her.

"These Vermont winters will be the death of me," she always said, and, in the end, it was true. She was winter-killed, but part of it was the winter she carried in her own soul, wherever she was.

Yesterday before twilight, the sky darkened suddenly under a cloud, hurricane black, a flying cloud that sailed high over the mountains encircling the farm. A strange unease fell on man and beast and even on me, though I have seen hurricanes enough.

16

So the heavy sandstorms used to fall upon Peking.
But there was neither sand nor rain in yesterday's
cloud. A few drops fell from the swollen shape above
and then the wind hurried it on.

Whatever the wind was, it blew the darkness away
and today the valley lies under a scintillating sun and
the warmth of it draws the mists again from the melting snow.

I dread the spring this year. I try not to look at the
clock. It is useless now to watch and wait for the postman. I shall never get another letter from Gerald. I
tell myself that every day. When Matt brought in the
mail this morning, I did not turn my head. "Put it on
the desk in the office," I said. But I went to look, just
the same, knowing there was no letter.

So I was busy, for we have the orchard to prune
before the sap begins to run in the sugar bush. We
raise good apples, old-fashioned and sound. The cellar is still stocked with them, although I have been
giving them away all winter. My favorites are the
pound apples, each weighing a pound, or very nearly,
red-skinned and crisp and a nice balance between sour
and sweet. When I bite into one I remember that
Gerald does not like apples. Chinese apples are pithy
and tasteless, but even our good American apples
could not tempt him. He came sometimes to help us
pick the apples but I never saw him eat one. Instead
he talked of pears. Yet once when I brought him a
plate of Bartletts he did not finish even a pear.

"They are soft," he said. "The pears in Peking are
as crisp as celery and full of clear juice."

"Then they are not pears," I said to tease him.

"Wait and see," he said.

For by then we knew we would be married as soon

17

as he had his doctor's degree. And when I did eat Peking pears they were different indeed, indescribable and delicious, pears certainly, but not American in taste or texture. At first I thought they were plucked before they were ripe, as the Chinese harvest their peaches, preferring a slightly green taste to the mellow sweet of ripeness. But the pears were ripe and they held their freshness all through the winter.

. . . We have pruned all day, Matt and I. He is a silent fellow, a Vermonter, lank and lean, his teeth gone too early from a wretched diet which nevertheless he will not improve. He looks upon my brown breads and green salads with distaste and refusal and though I press him to share my luncheon, he sits apart and munches what he calls lunch meat between two huge slabs of the cheap bread which I consider not bread but a solidified foam of white flour and water. Matt knows of my years in China and doubtless he wonders about Gerald but he never asks me a question that does not pertain to the farm. Save for this, his conversation consists of bits of bad news from the valley. Thus today I heard that the deep quarrel between young Tom Mosser and his wife has now reached the point of blows.

"He took a knife to her—not the blade, though," Matt said.

"What then?" I inquired.

"The handle," he said. "It was made of horn. He dug it in her."

"Where?" I inquired.

"Buzzim," he said briefly.

Bosom? Mollie Mosser has a big rich bosom and she wears her sweaters too tight. I did not continue the conversation.

"I want to finish the orchard before Rennie comes home from school," I said. And we went back to work.

And so, while my thoughts wander far from my Vermont hillside, I prune my apple trees, remembering that fruit is borne on the small and twiggy branches, and never on the bold young growth. Saw and shears I can use well enough, and I take the large branches first, cutting upwards for an inch or two, lest the wood split. When the saw is sharp, my neighbors say, it is time to prune the fruit trees, a saying true enough, for during the winter, when the weather is not fit for outside work, I oil the tools and sharpen the saws and the scythe. I have an old-fashioned wheel of sandstone that does well for the larger tools, but the small ones I sharpen by hand against a strip of flint. And I have learned to prune severely. A close, clean cut heals soon—that I have learned. But I know that too deep a cut will never heal. The branch will bear no fruit.

Nothing can hold back the spring. It comes against my dread, and I watch the signs. Rennie asks me every few days, "Mother, no letter?"

I shake my head. "I am afraid it is getting difficult for your father," I say. "The anti-American feeling in China is growing under the skillful communist propaganda."

Rennie muses, "What is communism, really?"

"Who knows?" I reply. "It is what people make it." And I tell him of Karl Marx, the strange little man, long dead, who lived his narrow little life, and somehow managed by the power of his wayward brain to lay hold upon millions of human lives.

"Even our lives, Rennie," I said. "Because of him

we are separated, you from father and I from husband."

"And can my father not free himself?" he asked.

How could I answer this? "I suppose," I said, "that if our country, here, went communist we'd stay, believing in our past and in our future, and hoping that somehow we'd escape."

"And could we?" he persisted. "And can my father?"

"I don't know," I said.

"Nor I, Mother," he said. "And I don't know even if this is my country."

"It is yours because it is mine," I said. "And let that be the end of it."

It is not the end, as I well know. Rennie will have to choose his own country.

And sooner or later I shall have to tell him that I have his father's last letter upstairs, locked into the secret drawer of my mother's old desk, for there will be no more letters now.

But I put off the day. Rennie went on talking this evening after our supper, which we ate by the kitchen fire. It is an old chimney piece, used once for cooking, or so I suppose. A crane is built under it and a great pot hangs from the crane, in which I still heat water when electricity fails in a summer thunderstorm.

"I should think my father could get a letter to us somehow," Rennie continued.

"We do not know what rigors are imposed upon him," I replied. "It is dangerous for him that his father is American."

"Where is my grandfather MacLeod?" Rennie asked.

Rennie likes apples. I keep a wooden bowl of them on the kitchen table for our evenings and while he

20

talked he was biting deeply into the white flesh of a red Baldwin.

"He's in Kansas. We shall have to go and find him one of these days," I said. "And do you forget that you used to call him Baba?"

I should have been looking at seed catalogues, but I was doing nothing except stare into the fire. I had planned long ago to visit Gerald's father. It was one of my beloved's last requests to me that day when we stood on the dock in Shanghai.

"Go and see my father and take Rennie with you," Gerald bade me. "It will comfort him to see his grandson."

"Is that why you are sending us to America?" I demanded.

"One reason among others," he replied.

"In that case I will stay here," I retorted.

"You must go," Gerald said, "and Rennie must go with you."

And then reluctantly he said what we both knew and had never spoken aloud. "Your lives will not be safe here if you stay."

I saw him glance about him as he spoke the words. For the first time Gerald was afraid. He had gone through war and bombing without a qualm. If he had ever been afraid he had hid his fear so that it seemed not to exist. But this fear he could not hide.

"What of you?" I asked and certainly I was afraid.

"Half of me is Chinese," he said. "I shall make that serve."

"But will They?" I muttered. We were already calling the Communists "They."

"I shall become indispensable," he replied.

I wished with all my heart that this conversation

21

had taken place when we were alone, when we were at home in Peking, in our house, in our bedroom, the doors locked, the windows closed. Then I could have thrown myself on his breast and forced the truth from him. Yet when could one force anything from Gerald? He has a will, a logic, which he alone can wield. I was standing beside him that day on the dock, the wind blowing my hair, and I could only ask in a stupid low voice that conveyed no passion, "And why, Gerald, do you wish to make yourself indispensable here?"

"One has to choose," he said.

There was no time for more. The tug was waiting to take us to the ship, and in the silent crowd upon the small vessel it would not have been safe to talk. I kept thinking, I remember. When had it become dangerous to talk? At what moment had the people, and among them ourselves, ceased to be gay and communicative, hiding nothing from each other? When had they become silent and afraid? I do not know the moment. The change was gradual, but when it came it was absolute. And it had culminated in the silence between Gerald and me when we parted.

I cannot sleep the nights through. I get up and prowl about the house, careful not to wake Rennie. His ear is too quick toward me. He guesses that something is wrong, but still I do not tell him about the letter. He thinks I grieve because I have not heard from his father for so many months. He says to me, "Mother, I am sure there are many letters waiting in some forgotten place. You know how the postmen are over there. They sit down to eat a bowl of hot rice, or they lie under a tree to sleep."

Actually this is not true. The postal service to and from Peking was always excellent, and I suppose it is no worse now. It was organized by the English, who are always thorough. I smile when Rennie tries such comfort. I say, "Of course you are right, and I will not worry. No news is good news."

It is a true old proverb. How much better it would be now if I had not this letter lying like a live thing in the secret drawer of my desk! I have sealed it with red sealing wax, lest by some impossible chance Rennie might be rummaging one day and find it. And having sealed it, I swear to myself that even I will never read it again.

. . . Last night I was too lonely. Oh, there is a loneliness which befalls me now and then and it is something more than death. I am still a wife, but without my husband. When a man dies, his widow dies by so much, too, perhaps. If her love has been great enough, a part of her dies and it can never be reborn with another man. But I am not a widow. In the night I wait and I lie in my solitary bed and all my dreams fly across the sea, annihilating time and space to seek the beloved. I walk the well-known street to our gate. It is barred against petty thieves but, bodiless, I go through and cross the courtyard and enter the locked door. The gateman does not wake. He cannot hear me, nor could he prevent me if he did. There is my home. It is as I left it, believing that surely I would come back. Gerald and I cannot be parted. That is what I believed.

I said to the servants, "Keep everything as I have it."

"We will," they promised.

"Do not forget," I said. "Our master must have hot

23

food when he comes in at night, however late the hour."

"Never, never can we forget," they promised.

"I shall return," I said.

"Our mistress will return," they said.

Now, remembering, my soul passes swiftly through the rooms to the bedroom where Gerald lies asleep. Surely he lies asleep. Is he alone? Is he still alone?

My soul stands fearful at the door. In a moment it flies back to me here. What, what was the day when Gerald wrote the letter? Does the letter tell the day? I am not sure. Soul in my waiting body, I get out of bed and I open the secret drawer of the desk. It is I who break the seal I set. I read the opening words again.

"Let me tell you that I love only you."

I bend my head and weep. Is it not enough that he has written these words? What does it matter whether tonight he sleeps alone—or does not? I fold the letter, my heart unanswered, and I seal it once more and once more I put it away in the secret drawer in the locked box.

I cannot return to my bed. When a woman is widowed by death, does passion die? Or does the body live on, clamoring for what is buried in the grave? But Gerald is not dead. He lives in more than memory. He is there, in our house. He comes home at night, he eats and sleeps and wakes to rise again. He looks upon this same moon which shines outside my window now. The awareness of his body sets my blood mad. Desire reaches for him, claims him, for he is not dead but living. Surely, surely he knows. He knows that I stand here by the window, that I look out at the moon, rising above the mists of a spring night. I remember, I remember—

For it was in this house that we first consummated our eternal love. We were not yet married. I write it down. I have never told our heavenly secret, nor has he. I am sure he has not. He says he loves only me, whatever happens, and so he has not told. Say it may have been wrong, but I am glad now for what I chose to do. For Gerald, always too sensitive, was obsessed with a strange terror in those first days when he had barely spoken to me of love. He feared that I might be offended by his Chinese flesh. It is true that sometimes he looks more Chinese than American.

I cried out against him. "Oh, darling, how silly you are!"

I was saying "darling" long before he could bring himself to speak the word. When he began to call me by endearing names, it was not easily at any time and in the presence of others, never.

I remember the look in his grave dark eyes. "I can live without your love," he said, "but I could not live if, having had it, I should lose it. This is why I dare not ask you to marry me."

It was true. He had not asked me, and he refused to let me say we were engaged.

"I shall always love you," I cried, impetuous.

"You do not know," he said. "You cannot be sure. The flesh has a will of its own."

It was on such a night as this, a moonlight night, that we spoke. The spring was late that year and we had lingered under the birch trees to be alone and away from my mother, and I was cold and he opened his coat and put it about my shoulders and I walked in his shelter.

"It is you who are not sure," I told him.

And then I pondered how to make him sure.

"If you think I shall not love you for some hidden reason I do not now know," I told him, "then come to my room tonight. Let us hide nothing from each other. Let us make sure before we marry."

I felt him quiver. I knew he was shocked and yet moved.

"No," he said, "I cannot do that."

It was June before he was willing. He had his degree then from Harvard. My mother came to Commencement and I was singing proud to hear the honors he received. "*Summa cum laude*—" the words were spoken again and yet again. My mother was warmer than I had ever seen her toward him when he came striding toward us, still in his cap and gown. There was no man there to equal him in beauty. For the moment his reserve was gone. He was triumphant and happy and he caught our hands, my mother's and mine.

"Thank you for coming," he said. "Without you, I should have had no family. I'd have been lonely."

"Congratulations," my mother said. She pressed his hand in both hers, but I stood tiptoe and kissed his cheek. It was the first time I had kissed him before my mother and he blushed and glanced at her and smiled when she did not reprove me.

We had dinner together that night, the three of us, at some Chinese restaurant in Boston, where he had already ordered our meal, and my mother condescended to taste one strange dish after another. But I ate everything, liking all, and Gerald laughed at me and loved me and I knew it, in spite of his careful reserve.

He came home with us the next day, and by evening we were in the house, the three of us. It was a clear night, I remember, the air cool and sweet as only the air of the mountains can be, and my mother said she was tired, and she went early to bed. Gerald and I sat late on the stone terrace my father had built the summer before he died, and somehow I fell to talking about him, and telling Gerald about him. "I wish he could know about you," I said.

"What about me?" Gerald asked. He held my hand now, his hand cool and firm, and mine much warmer, always, and clinging to his.

"I wish, I wish my father could know the man who is to be my husband," I said.

A bold thing I was, but I knew what I wanted and I knew that Gerald loved me. Why he had not asked me to marry him I did not know but there would be time enough to find out, for we were in love.

He sat silent for a time, holding my hand. Then he rose from the bench where we were sitting and he drew me up to him and kissed me as never before had he kissed me.

It was I who broke away from that long and penetrating kiss. "Now we are engaged," I whispered.

He held me against him. "If only I could be sure—"

"Then let us be sure," I said.

The night turned suddenly grave. We were both silent. We sat down again and in the deepening darkness he talked to me of Peking and his childhood home there, and for the first time he spoke of his mother. She had not been a beautiful woman, he said. Her face was plain, but she had extraordinary grace of carriage and manner. Her hands were delicate and always fragrant. He remembered their scent when she smoothed his cheeks.

"Chinese women do not kiss their children as western women do," he said. "They nuzzle them and smell them when they are babies. When I grew out of babyhood she smoothed my cheeks with both her hands. Her palms were soft and sweet."

"Who was she," I asked, "and how did she come to marry your father?"

"I think, but I do not know," he said, "that my father was disappointed in love. The American woman he wanted to marry would not go to China with him, or was forbidden to go by her parents. She was not strong enough to disobey them, I suppose, and so she refused my father. In pride he went to China alone and he lived alone for ten years of his life. And then, you know how the Chinese are—" He caught himself. "No, how can you know how the Chinese are? Well, they think every man and woman must marry for it is what Heaven ordains, and there can be no health in a people unless there is health in the individual man and woman. So Chinese friends besought my father to marry, and his best friend, who is my foster father, my uncle Han Yu-ren, offered him his sister. Thus she became my mother. She was not young. She was, in a way, a widow. The man to whom she had been betrothed as a child, by her parents, died a week before the wedding. Had she been less independent, I suppose she would have followed tradition and never married. She might even have become a nun."

"She was willing to marry an American?" I asked.

"That is what drew my father to her," Gerald said. "Most young Chinese women would not have accepted a foreign man. They would have cried out that foreigners are hairy and have a smell and are altogether repulsive in—in—intimacy." He stumbled over the word.

"Had she seen your father?" I asked. I was fascinated by the Chinese woman who was Gerald's mother.

"Once," he said, "when my father visited his friend's house, she was in the main hall and though she left immediately, she saw him. He did not notice her."

"Your father is very handsome," I reminded him. He had once shown me his father's picture.

"Yes."

"Were they happy?" I persisted.

He considered the question. "They had a measured happiness. It was impossible to be altogether unhappy with my mother. She was never gay but never sad, and she created order wherever she was."

"Is order so important?" I cried. For I am not orderly by nature. There is always something more important than putting things in place.

"There is no dignity to life except with order," Gerald said.

We talked thus slowly and thoughtfully, our hands clasped. The moon was high and the mountains were clear against the sky. And while our minds ranged across the seas, we knew what the night held. It is Gerald's way not to speak when he feels most deeply, but the quality of his silence, the luminous look of his eyes, the controlled gentleness of his voice, all betray the depths.

We heard the grandfather clock in the hall strike twelve and we rose together and went into the house and up the stairs. The guest room is at the head of the stairs and we paused. The house was still, and the door to my mother's room was closed. The night had come.

"I will leave my door open," I said softly.

He took me in his arms and kissed me again, not passionately but gently and with deep tenderness. Then he went into the guest room and shut the door.

And I went to my own room and closed the door behind me while I prepared myself. A calm happiness pervaded me. I understood now why marriage is a sacrament. In this mood I bathed my body and brushed my long hair and put on a fresh white nightgown. Then I opened my door. His was still closed. While I waited I sat on the deep window seat beside the window and gazed over the mountains that surrounded us. In an hour, less or more, I heard his footstep. I turned and saw him in the doorway. He stood there, wrapped in his dressing gown of blue Chinese silk. We looked at each other. Then he held out his arms and I went into them.

I read novels sometimes in the winter evenings while Rennie studies his books for school. The novels describe again and again the act of physical love between man and woman. I read these descriptions, wondering at their monotony and their dullness. The act of love can, then, be meaningless! I wonder at such degradation. And then I realize that it is degraded because the two who perform it are degraded, and I wonder if I had not married Gerald whether I, too, might have been caught in that prison of stupid repetition until what was designed as the supreme act of communion and creation becomes merely a physical function. I thank the beloved who saved me from such desecration. I understand now the desolate look in women's eyes that often I see. For it is the man and not the woman who is the more responsible for the beauty or the horror of the moment when the two meet. When a woman receives in exaltation and is given in haste and selfishness she is desecrated. She has been used as a clay pot may be used, and she is more than clay. She is spirit.

I do not know who taught Gerald this high truth, but he knew it when he came to me. Perhaps his mother told him. There was something clear and free between them, something that he has not shared with me because it belongs to her. There has never been any confusion in Gerald's mind between wife and mother. He wished no mothering from me and he made no Freudian connection between me and his mother. There were no repressions in him. He created the physical relationship between us with delicate artistry, satisfying himself in so doing and me. How he did it is not something to be described. It is to be remembered by him and by me. It will be my duty to explain to Rennie, when he marries, his responsibility to beauty.

That night, so long ago now, when Gerald entered my room for the first time, he came in beauty and what he conveyed to me was the beauty which is the stuff of true romance. And so it continued through the years of our life together. Never in haste and always with tenderness, he made me his love. Now, without him, I have this, my memory.

I find I must not dwell upon memory or it becomes unbearable. If Gerald were dead, then memory would be all that I have. The gift would be completed, the life finished. But he lives. Because he lives I too must live, though memory remains between us like a cord, so that I cannot be separated from him. Yet we are apart in time and space, and time must be filled and space occupied.

I am thankful that the sap has begun to run in the sugar bush for I have no choice now but to be busy. Rennie has permission to stay out of school for a few days. His grades are high and his teacher says it will give her a chance to help some of the dull ones. The three of us, Matt, Rennie and I, work from dawn to dark and at night I am too tired to dream. I think of cutting off my long hair but today when I was impatient because it fell down my back, the hairpins failing to hold in the wind, Rennie protested.

"I shall certainly cut this off," I cried, seizing the long tail of sand-blond hair and twisting it hard against my head.

The wind carried my words to Rennie and he cupped his hands and called to me, "You shall not, either!

Later when we were eating our luncheon I asked him why he would not let me cut my hair and he said because he did not like a short-haired woman.

"I am not a woman," I said. "I am only your mother."

"Short-haired mother, then," he retorted and laughed at me.

I wonder if Gerald laughed as easily when he was a boy. There is no one to tell me. I shall never know.

It is strange how devious is the human heart. I had no sooner written those words than I thought, there is Gerald's father. He will remember. Out of that chance thought there grew a plan and so quickly that it must have lain ready to be discovered. As soon as this sugaring is finished, Rennie and I will go and find Gerald's father. When we were carrying the buckets to the trees on the north side of the sugar bush, where they are always late, with all the wile of a serpent I said to Rennie the next day:

"Rennie, how would you like to have your MacLeod grandfather come and live with us? Another man in the house—"

"I think I remember him," Rennie said.

Gerald's father left Peking before the Japanese entered. He said quite simply that he could not bear to see it, and he bought a steamship ticket for San Francisco. From there he went to a small town in Kansas, Little Springs. I have no idea how he lives now. He has written to us once, soon after we came to Vermont, and wanted news of Gerald, which I gave, telling him all I could. He has not replied.

"Well?" I said to Rennie.

"I shall have to think about it," Rennie said. He is prudent, this boy, and to that extent is not my son. Perhaps my mother has given him prudence. If so, it is not the niggardly prudence she had. Rennie is cautious and careful. He thinks, but when he has decided he is generous.

The days passed while he thought, and a day at sugaring is long and short at the same time. It is hard work but we are fortunate. My father tapped the trees and laid pipes throughout the bush, and those pipes run into three main large pipes. By force of gravity the sap is conveyed to a small but fairly modern sugar house in the valley and near our house. All the years I was growing up and going to college, my father's ingenuity went into such matters and now Rennie and I, with Matt's help, make sugar with twice the ease that our neighbors do. They see and wonder and sometimes give spare praise to my father, but none of them do likewise. They continue to carry buckets as they have always done and as their ancestors did. I used to be impatient with them until I lived in Peking and learned the value of ancestors to a family. I am glad that through his Chinese grandmother Rennie has ancestors for a thousand years behind him. I have been able to give him only a scant two hundred years of English men and women.

Sap runs fast in the warm sunlit days into the sugar house. When that begins then Rennie and Matt do the outside work and I stay in the sugar house. The milking gets done anyhow and we eat from our stores of food, cooking no more than to heat what is already prepared in the glass jars of summertime and harvest.

We had no time to talk, for we dropped into sleep immediately after supper, Rennie's cheeks burned with wind and snow and mine with fire, and while we rubbed them with oil we all but fell asleep. Today, however, winter has returned. The pipes are frozen and the roads are drifting with deepening snow. We can rest, Rennie and I, and Matt has taken over the sugar house for the time being. We dallied over our kitchen breakfast and Rennie picked up his first book in days, for it is a Saturday. I interrupted him.

"Rennie, have you thought about your grandfather coming to live with us?"

He looked up from the window seat where he was lying, feet against the wall, and the book propped on his breast.

"I have thought," he said. "I'd like it." And he went back to his book.

Son of Gerald! He has thought, in silence he has decided, and it is as good as done. When the dishes were washed I went upstairs to consider the room the grandfather would have. The house is too big for us. My father had a mania for space. He wanted many rooms, none small. The house he left behind him could have a dozen children. Half-stone, half-timber, it stands facing the south and the valley. Every summer someone from New York or Chicago wants to buy it from me. I am offered a fortune large enough so that we need never sugar again. And I always refuse.

So now I walk the wide upstairs hall and reflect upon the rooms. I choose the corner at south and east. Rennie has the southwest room, because he likes to sleep on holidays and does not want the wakening sun. But an old man will not sleep late and this is the room. It is square, as all the bedrooms are, it has four windows, weather-stripped for winter, and a fireplace stands between the two to the east. Deep window sills and seats beneath them, a floor of wide pine planks, walls papered a faded pink, and there it is. My mother chose this room when she was old and her furniture is here, Victorian walnut, and the white ruffled curtains that she made and hung. The bed is absurdly large, the headboard high and scrolled and the footboard solid. It is a good room for an old gentleman. There is even a desk. My mother had my father's small rolltop brought here when he died, and I can see still her sitting before it and writing letters, everything in order in the pigeonholes. My father kept it filled to overflowing and never tidied. It will be pleasant to see someone sitting there again.

And then I face myself. I want Gerald's father here so that I can talk about his son. I need to know much I do not know. I thought I knew Gerald, my husband —heart, mind and body—and so I did in the days when

I saw him with my living eyes. But now I have only the eyes of memory and there is much I cannot see because I do not know. And somebody must tell me, lest my life be stopped at the heart.

We could not go until the sugaring was over. It was interrupted by an ice storm. In March, midseason, a warm rain poured upon us from a low gray sky. We were frightened lest the sap cease to flow, the trees deceived by seeming spring. Then sudden winds blew gusts of cold southward from Canada, and the rain froze upon the trees. Sap was assured, but alas, winds crashed the big trees. Sleepless in the night I heard the crack of breaking branches, sharp as gun shots, and almost as dreadful. In the morning the sun shone again and Rennie and I walked through the sugar bush to see what we had lost. Icicles of frozen sap hung from the ends of the broken branches and melting in the sun they dripped their sweetness upon the earth below. I detest waste and here was waste not only for us now but for the trees which had during the summer stored sunshine through their leaves. The hot summer sunshine creates starch in the leaf cells, and the cool spring sunshine changes the starch to sugar, to be used by trees and by us. Then Rennie reminded me that a tree is prudent and never gives up all its sugar.

"At least we can enjoy the beauty," I said. So we stood on the top of the mountain behind our house and surveyed the glittering landscape.

Such events, such scenes, distract me and I record them. I do not complain. For six weeks of hard work, we have now a hundred gallons of amber-clear maple syrup, to be boiled later into sugar. I am particular about the color of the syrup. The first run is sweetest and best, and when the buds begin to swell the season is over. The late sap is thick and strong and will not make good sugar.

When the buds began to swell in April, I told Matt that he must tend the spring ploughing alone, or else hire John Stark from down the valley to help him, for Rennie and I were going to Kansas. We would be back, I told him, before the seeds he planted could sprout.

"I may bring my husband's father," I said to prepare him.

Matt does not speak unless he must. He looked at me, his face carefully blank.

"You don't know him," I went on, "but he's alone and if he needs us, he'll live with us."

A strange look crept over Matt's dun-colored face. He no longer believed in the existence of Gerald.

"You've seen Gerald," I reminded him. Matt has worked here as long as I can remember.

"I've sort of forgot his looks," he said.

I opened the table drawer and took out the silver-framed picture of my husband. In the evenings I take it out, when Rennie and I sit here at our work, he at his books, I at my sewing, and then there are three of us. I cannot bear to look at it in the daytime, for I am reminded constantly that Gerald is thousands of miles away, across the widest ocean on the globe. But in the evening he comes close. I see him sitting in our house in Peking, thinking of us. I hope and pray he thinks of us.

"This is he," I said to Matt.

He took the framed photograph in his two hands and stared at Gerald's handsome face.

"Still looks like a nice feller," he said cautiously and handed the picture to me again and went away.

At least he knows now that Gerald lives, and he will tell the other valley people and perhaps the reserve which they show me will yield to a warmer atmosphere. My grandfather did not belong to the valley and my parents were summer people first, and I cannot expect in one generation to be considered a valley woman. Perhaps they suspect Rennie of being a misdemeanor.

In April, the leaves of the maples being in bud, Rennie and I set forth on our journey. We had discussed going in the car and then had rejected the idea. Better to go by train, better and quicker, and easier, too, for an old man who might be returning with us. So far as I was concerned, he was coming. Only his own will against it could prevent his return to the family.

I tried to create his image for Rennie as the days passed by, plains and mountains flying across the windows of the train, but it was dim even in my own mind. I saw everyone through the bright mists of my love for Gerald. I am one of the fortunate women who marry their first love. I have no memory of any other. The first run of maple syrup, John Burroughs says, is like first love, "always the best, always the fullest, always the sweetest, while there is a purity and delicacy of flavor about the sugar that far surpasses any subsequent yield."

"Your grandfather," I told Rennie, "is tall and very thin and aristocratic in his appearance. Remember that he comes from Virginia. It is a wonder that he ever married a Chinese lady."

Rennie withdrew by the slightest movement. He does not wish nowadays to talk about his Chinese grandmother. I suspect the prejudices of his school-fellows may be creeping into his soul. If so, then Gerald's father will help me.

"Your grandfather has dark hair and dark eyes, like your father," I went on. "His hair is probably silver-white by now. Can you remember him at all?"

"I don't remember," Rennie said stubbornly. Whenever we speak of the life we lived in Peking he does not remember. He wants to be American.

"Ah well, when you see your grandfather, it will all come back to you," I said. But I do not know if this is true.

The landscape passes too quickly by the window. Some day I shall travel slowly over the miles we whirl over now. I would like to stop at every village and town and walk on the country roads that wind away from us in an instant. I want to feel my roots go deep again. Last night in my berth I pulled the curtain aside and gazed out into the moonlight. I did not know where we were, what state, what county. I knew only my nation, and this so vast that within its endless borders even I can be a stranger. I ought not to blame Gerald that he does not come here, lest he be exiled.

I wept on his bosom that last night we had to-gether in the Shanghai hotel. "Why won't you come with me?" I sobbed. "What is it here that you love better than your wife?"

"No one and nothing," he said. "Consider, my Eve, that if I leave China now it would be forever. And I'd be a stranger in America."

"I'd be there," I cried.

"Though you were there," he said gravely.

I remember everything he ever said to me, not in a

continual stream of memory, but interposed into my present life. Thus at midnight, in the vastness of the land over which we sped, I felt myself a stranger, and I remembered what he said.

We have found Gerald's father. He is living alone in a shack, a hut, at the edge of a cluster of one-story houses in western Kansas. Little Springs is a small town, less than a town. It is on the high plains, half-way to the mountains. It was easy to find him, for when we asked at the station everybody knew him in a strange respectful doubtful sort of way.

"MacLeod? That's the old gentleman." This was the shirt-sleeved man at the ticket window, talking around the cud of tobacco in his mouth.

He directed us to the far end of the one street and a mile beyond it in a one-room unpainted house we found Gerald's father. The door was open, although the air is chill here, even in April, and he was sitting inside at a rough table, wearing, of all things, his old padded Chinese robe and reading a Chinese book. When he saw us he got to his feet in his formal fashion and stood there smiling. He has let his beard grow and his hair is too long. Both are silver-white. He is terribly thin and his eyes are huge. I never knew before how much he looks like Gerald. I flew to him and put my arms around him.

"Baba—why on earth are you here?"

Baba was what I had always called him. It is easier to say than Father. And hearing the name now, he lifted his bent head, he saw me and recognized me, strangely without surprise, as though he did not know where he was. He did not embrace me but he did not push my arms away. He said in a mild distant voice,

"I was taken ill on the train and they put me off here, and here perforce I stopped. There is no reason for me to live one place rather than another."

How selfishly Gerald and I lived on in the house in Peking in those perilous prewar days! We knew we were selfish, and yet we clutched every doomed hour of happiness. Yet it is also true that we believed anyone who reached America had reached heaven. We thought of Baba as safe merely because he had left the troubled provinces of China. We had a few letters from him, placid letters, saying that he was comfortable and we were not to worry about him, that he had found friends. And beset with our own worries, in wars and dangers, we simply forgot him.

Baba was looking at Rennie and I stepped back.

"You remember your grandson," I said.

He put out his hand, a frail big hand, and I nodded to Rennie to bid him come forward and he obeyed shyly.

"Gerald's son?" the old man inquired.

"Of course," I said. How much does he remember and how much is forgotten? Rennie was a child of six when he saw him last.

"Yes, yes," the grandfather murmured. "Sit down, sit down."

There were not two other seats and Rennie sat on the edge of the table and I upon a stool.

"Baba, how do you live?" I asked.

"I live," he said vaguely. "They bring me food, a woman cleans my house and washes my clothes. I don't need money. People are kind here."

He does not know where he is. He simply got off the train when his money gave out and somebody let

41

him have this house. It belongs, I can guess, to a larger house a half-mile or so up the road.

"I have money," he was saying. He opened the drawer in the table and took out a small parcel wrapped in a piece of yellow Chinese silk and opening it he showed me five one-dollar bills. Then he wrapped it up again and put it in the drawer.

Rennie and I looked at each other. If we had any doubts they were gone. We agreed, without words. We must take Baba home with us, and without delay. There was one train east and one train west each day.

"Have you had your luncheon, Baba?" I asked. If we made haste we could still catch the eastward train.

"I think so," he replied.

"What did you eat?"

He got up slowly and went to an old-fashioned ice-box in the corner and opened it. I looked inside and saw a half-empty bottle of milk, a pat of butter, three eggs and a small meat pie, a wedge of which had been cut out.

Then we sat down again. Rennie was standing in the door now, looking over the rising plains.

"Let's get going," he said.

I turned to Baba. "Will you come and live with us?"

He was sitting by the table again and now he carefully closed the cloth-bound Chinese book.

"Do you wish me to come and live with you?" he inquired.

"More than anything," I said.

"Where is Gerald?" he asked.

"He is still in Peking."

"Will he return?"

"I—hope so."

"Someone is coming," Rennie said.

The someone was a man. He was walking toward us in long strides and in a moment was at the door, a man past youth and not yet middle-aged, tall and square shouldered, sandy haired, his skin the color of his hair, a wind-blown Western face.

"I came down to see what was going on," he said in a hearty voice. "I keep an eye on my old neighbor."

"Are you the owner of this shack?" I asked.

"Yes—it's on my farm. My father raised sheep and this was the herder's shack."

"It was good of you to take my father-in-law into shelter," I said.

"I don't know what to think of folks who let an old man wander around alone," he said severely.

"We had no idea—" I began and stopped. How could I explain to this forthright man how it was that an old man could arrive alone in an unknown place and stay there? How could I explain Peking, or even China? As well try to explain a distant planet!

"Now that we have found him," I said, "we will take him home." Then I remembered. "I am Mrs. Gerald MacLeod. This is my son, Rennie."

"I'm Sam Blaine," he said. But he was looking at Rennie. He was thinking that Rennie looked "different." Who, he was thinking, are these people?

"Where do you come from?" he asked.

"We live in Vermont," I said.

"Where's your husband?"

I hesitated. It would be easier to say that Gerald was dead than to explain where he was and why. To say that he wanted to stay in Communist China would be to bring down suspicion upon us all.

"He is abroad," I said.

Sam Blaine leaned against the door and looked us over thoughtfully. Then he spoke to Baba.

"Old friend, you recognize this lady and the boy?"

Baba nodded peacefully. "She is my son's wife. The boy is Gerald's son."

"You want to go with them?"

"I'll go with them."

"Not unless you want to—I'll look after you if you want to stay."

"I will go," Baba said.

"Well—" The tall American was doubtful. "If you say so—"

"If we hurry we can still catch the afternoon train," I said.

"I'll fetch my car," he said. "He hasn't much to pack. Where is your luggage?"

"We had left it at the station," Rennie told him.

"I'll be back in fifteen minutes," Sam Blaine said and strode off.

I saw now that Rennie was in distress. He was looking at his grandfather and making up his mind whether to speak.

"Well?" I inquired.

"Are you going to take him on the train wearing that Chinese gown?" my son demanded.

Baba surveyed himself. "It's a very nice gown," he observed. "I bought it in Peking. The silk is still good. It is warm and soft."

"Mother!" Rennie cried.

"Baba, we will take the gown with us," I said. "But perhaps it will be best if we find your coat. Americans are not used to people who look different."

The gentle old man said nothing to this and Rennie was already reaching behind a curtain which hung

44

against the wall and served as a closet. He produced the dark-gray suit in which Baba had left Peking, and the dark overcoat Gerald had bought him at the English tailor shop in the old Legation Quarter. They looked very little worn. Evidently Baba had lived in the Chinese silk gowns he had folded so carefully into his suitcase. He let Rennie help him into the gray suit and we put on his overcoat and found his black homburg hat and he stood quite beautiful and patient under our appraisal. Nothing disturbs him. He is gentle, he is obedient. Has something gone wrong with his mind? I cannot tell. I was not sure he knew what was happening to him. He simply gave himself into our hands.

Dust and noise outside the door announced that Sam Blaine had returned. I had packed the suitcase and Rennie led his grandfather to the car. Sam Blaine leaped out, his long legs curiously dexterous, and in a half-minute we were in the car, the dust flying behind us. The car itself was monstrous, red and chrome, enormous in size and as comfortable as a bed.

"I have never seen such a car," I said. For I was in the front seat, and Rennie and Baba were behind.

"Made to order," Sam Blaine said. "My order."

He drove fast and I stopped talking. I shall never grow used to speed. Years of riding in rickshaws and mule carts have reduced my tempo permanently, perhaps. We reached the station in time for the train, and Baba, supported by Rennie and Sam Blaine, was lifted up the steps.

"Good-bye, ma'am," Sam Blaine said, and wrenched my hand. "You might write me, and tell me how the old man makes it."

"I will," I promised.

The train was already moving and the porter pulled me into the door and locked it. We settled ourselves into the compartment, Baba, Rennie and I. Then I was conscious of pain somewhere and it was in my hand, the one Sam Blaine had held in his crushing grip.

Matt has dug the garden and ploughed our fields. I am experimenting this year by putting the land into hay, permanent hay. Grass farming, I believe, is the only answer to our short season in these mountains. A hundred years ago men made fields among the rocks and tried to grow grain and their fields have returned to wilderness. Eighteen thousand folk, the old records say, once gathered on the side of Mount Stratton to hear Daniel Webster speak. I doubt eighteen hundred could gather now were Daniel Webster to rise even from the grave. They have gone away, those folk, and their children and children's children are living their lives in strange and distant places. They went away in search of home, even as I have returned to find my home.

For I am beginning to know that I shall never return to the house in Peking. It must cease to exist for me, though it stands as it has stood for centuries, a house encompassed by walls, and the gate in those walls is of heavy cedar, bound in solid brass. In and out of the gate the beloved comes and goes, but my place is empty, forever. My roots there must die. I have returned to the land of my fathers. I ask myself if I should read Gerald's letter aloud to Baba, so that he may know what has happened to me and to Gerald, and then cannot bear the thought of sharing my secret, not today. For this is our wedding day, Gerald's and mine, the fifteenth day of May, and I have spent it in the fields, seeding grass for permanent cover, leaving Matt to clean the barn and milk the cows. While I worked without ceasing I have been remembering.

Twenty years ago today Gerald and I were married quietly in the big living room, and no one was there except my mother and her brother and his wife. I do not know what has become of my uncle and aunt. When I went to China with Gerald, I was drawn into its vast slumberous life. I felt at home there as everyone does. I do not know why it is so. People came to visit Peking and stayed to live out their lives. In those days Gerald explained everything to me which I did not understand, he told me what people said on the streets as we passed. And because nothing was strange to him, nothing was strange to me.

I tell myself that now all is changed, even in that eternal city. The long slumber is over. A terrible new energy possesses the people. I tell myself that they do not want me there. Even though they love me, for I cannot believe that my friend and next-door neighbor, Sumei, does not love me any more in her heart, not when I remember how we nursed our babies together and talked and laughed and told each other what we had paid at the markets that day for eggs and fish and fruits. I cannot believe that old Madame Li does not love me any more, she who often drew me down to sit beside her so that she could smooth my hands with hers. These were my friends, I love them still and surely they love me. They would say as Gerald says to me in the letter, "I love you and will always love you, but—"

How can there be buts if love continues? That is

the question I cannot answer. And silence lies between us.

. . . When I came in to make supper Baba was enjoying the late sun on the kitchen terrace. He wears his Chinese gown every day, and he sits and reads his few old Chinese books and seldom speaks. I do not know what he thinks about. The doctor in our valley, Dr. Bruce Spaulden, tells me he has had a shock of some kind, a stroke, perhaps, when he was alone there in the shack in Little Springs.

"Can such a thing happen and no one know?" I asked.

Bruce Spaulden is a good man and a good doctor, very tall, an honest face, strong features. What else? I have not had time to know him well. Rennie and I are never ill, we have not been in need of him.

"Such things do happen," he said. He is an earnest fellow. "There's nothing to do," he said. "Simply take care of him as you are doing." He is never in a hurry, but not communicative. He had come to examine Baba at my request, because I do not understand this old man I have taken into my house. He is not the man I remember as Gerald's father. In Peking Baba's mind was keen, cultivated, witty, the mind of a scholar. I was afraid of him and charmed by him when I went to live in his house with Gerald. He knew everything and information flowed from him with pure naturalness, never with condescension. The subtle mellowing and maturing which China seems always to leave upon all who give themselves to her had reached perfection in him.

"Gerald, how can I ever please your father?" I cried on the first night we spent in the Peking house.

"My darling," Gerald said, "you need not try to

please him. He is already pleased. In the first place he likes everyone, in his own fashion. In the second place, he is delighted with you because you don't pretend. Neither does he. You can take each other as you are."

Baba has still that naturalness and he has his old-fashioned courtesy. Without one word to Rennie he teaches his grandson the manners he is losing since he became an American schoolboy. Baba will not sit down at the table until I am seated. He is careful to tell me when he goes for one of his short walks into the sugar bush and to find me and tell me again when he returns. He loves to walk slowly in the shade of the maples and among the ferns now unrolling their fronds beneath the trees. Matt and Rennie keep the bush cleaned of small stuff and the ferns come up in a carpet of jade green.

Baba reports to me each small beauty that he sees, and this makes our conversation, now that Rennie comes late because of baseball at school. Baba sits in the kitchen with me and we talk. Oh, but it is different talk now. He is not childish—no, not that—but something has gone from him. The old scintillating wit is silent, the mind rests. He is sweet and gentle and easy to live with, and he does not complain. He does not long for his old life. Somehow he knows it is no more. He simply accepts his daily bread. I am not sure he knows where he is. I think he forgets at times who I am. He looks at Rennie now and then with strange thoughtfulness, but he does not speak. I feel he is inquiring of himself whether this is Gerald or Gerald's son, or even sometimes, whether he knows him. . . . No, it would be cruel to show him Gerald's letter. I could not explain it.

Tonight, when we had eaten our supper, Rennie was off again to go with his friends to a motion picture. It is Saturday and I allow the privilege, especially as school reports came in this week and Rennie's is good.

So Baba and I were alone and I lit the lamp. I took up my knitting and sat down by the table and Baba remained in his armchair. And I, of course, while I knitted a red sweater for Rennie, could not but think of Gerald. Never before, in the years since we parted, had our anniversary passed without a letter from him. Somehow or other he managed to get a letter through Hongkong to reach me in time for this night, and so to renew his love. I have the letters upstairs, in my sandalwood box. On other years I have read them all again, in full faith that some day our separation would end. I do not know whether I shall have the courage to read them tonight.

Baba does not speak unless I speak first. He sits quietly and watches me with patient eyes. Tonight I could not bear this and so I began to talk.

"Baba, tell me, can you remember when you married Gerald's mother?"

He did not look startled. It was almost as if he had been thinking of her at that moment.

"I do remember her," he said. "Her name was Ai-lan. Her surname was Han. She was a good woman and a good wife."

"How did you come to marry her?"

He pondered this, his eyes vague. "I cannot remember," he said. "I was adviser then to the Young Emperor. My friend, Han Yu-ren, suggested her to me. He thought I was lonely, and he had a sister younger than I. She was Ai-lan."

"And were you lonely?" I asked.

He considered this. "I suppose so, or I would not have married."

"Were you in love, Baba?" I asked.

Again the pause. I looked at him, and he made a picture as he sat there in my father's old brown leather armchair, the light of the lamp falling upon his Chinese robe of crimson silk, his hands folded upon his lap, and his white hair and beard shining, his eyes dark and troubled. He was trying to think.

"Never mind, Baba," I said. "It was all so long ago."

"It is not that I do not wish to tell you," he said. "I am trying to remember. I think I was in love. I feel that I was in love, but not with Ai-lan. I was in love with someone else. It is she I am trying to remember."

"Was she a Chinese lady?" I asked, knowing she was not.

"Not Chinese," he said.

"Then what?"

"That is what I cannot remember."

"Her name?"

"I cannot remember her name."

Oh, what a thing to say! My knitting fell from my hands. To be in love and then to pass beyond even the memory of the beloved's name! Can this happen? Could Gerald one day, in Peking, years hence, forget even my name?

Baba was still remembering, his mind searching the past. He began to talk again. "I was lonely, I believe, because the one—that one whose name I cannot remember—did not return my love. Yes, I do remember loving someone who did not love me. I had proposed marriage, perhaps—well, I do not know. But certainly

51

I was alone and when Yu-ren said to me that he had a sister, I thought it might be a good thing to be married to a Chinese lady. She could help me, I thought, in my work with the Chinese."

I took up my knitting again. "Strange, was it not, that a Chinese lady should be unmarried?"

He said quite easily now, "She had been betrothed and her fiancé had died. There was a cholera epidemic, I believe. I think Yu-ren said he had died when she was quite young—perhaps fifteen. Yes, I am sure about that. She was twenty-five when we were married and I was thirty."

"Strange, was it not, for her to be willing to marry a foreigner?" I had somehow opened a door into Baba's mind and I pressed my advantage for the most selfish reasons. I wanted to know Gerald's mother. Baba had never spoken of her in the old days. There was not even a picture of her in the Peking house. And Gerald could not bear to speak of her. He loved her painfully well, and I did not know why it was with pain.

The Vermont night was quiet about us, a lovely night, moonless and soft. May can be cold in our valley, or warm. Tonight was warm. I had closed the windows not against cold but against the moths drawn to the lamp. The house was silent. The day's work was done. I felt no barrier between Baba and me, and as though he felt none, either, he spoke with the simple words of a child, sometimes in English and sometimes in Chinese. It was strange and beautiful to hear the liquid tones of the ancient Peking language here in this room. What would my mother have thought! And how my father would have listened! And neither would have understood. But I understood. I am glad now that I learned Chinese. The hours I pored over the books with old Mr. Chen, the teacher Gerald found for me, are richly paid for to-night.

For here is the story Baba told me, sitting yonder in the brown armchair, his long pale hands folded one upon the other, his eyes fixed on my face some-times, and sometimes moving away to the darkening window. The story flowed from him as life came back to his memory, and he became someone else, not the scholar, all Virginian courtliness and Chinese grace, whom I had known as Gerald's father, but an old man reliving a handful of vivid years in his youth.

They had been married, he and Gerald's mother, ac-cording to the ancient Buddhist rites. Confucian and skeptic in their education, when death and marriage and birth took place the family returned, nevertheless, to their Buddhist traditions.

"And were her parents willing to accept an Amer-ican?" I asked Baba.

Her parents were dead, it seemed, and her elder brother, Han Yu-ren, was the head of the family. At first he could not persuade his sister. She had come to look upon herself as a widow, and she thought it un-chaste to marry. She had even considered becoming a Buddhist nun, as many young widows do in China, but her brilliant agnostic mind forbade this. She could not undergo a life of ritual in which she did not be-lieve. Much as a nun might have done, however, she lived in the Han household, pursuing her studies.

"Was she beautiful, Baba?"

He considered this for some time. "She was not," he said at last, "although there were times when she very nearly approached beauty."

"And these times?" It was impudent of me to ask the question, for might she not have been beautiful in love?

Baba was not distressed. He answered in the same tranquil manner. "She was beautiful when she read aloud to me the ancient poetry she enjoyed. This was a pleasure to her. And also she played quite well upon her lute when she sang and she had a sweet melancholy voice. When she had played in the evenings, she always wiped tears from her eyes. I do not know why she wept."

"After Gerald was born, was she happy?"

A vague trouble passed over Baba's face. "I do not know whether it can be called happiness. She was changed. She read no more poetry and she never again played her lute. Instead she became interested in the revolution. Until then she had paid no heed to political affairs. I do not remember that she ever read a newspaper before Gerald was born. But afterwards, I remember, she began to read new books and magazines. She became friendly, in a distant fashion, with Sun Yat-sen. I remember we quarreled over it."

"I cannot imagine you quarreling, Baba," I said.

He did not hear this, or he paid it no heed. "I did not like Sun Yat-sen. I distrusted him. I was then the adviser to the Throne, you understand. I believed that the old form of government was the best. Besides, Sun was not educated in the classics. He had been only to missionary schools."

I was astonished to hear Baba speak so well. Something of the man I had known appeared before me. I put down my knitting to watch and to listen while he went on.

"We differed, she and I. She, who had been reared

54

in every ancient tradition, was suddenly another woman than the one I had married. As a Chinese lady she had never left our house. Now, as the child grew out of babyhood, she began to go here and there and when I asked her where she went she said she went to meetings. This was how I knew she went to hear Sun Yat-sen. He was an upstart, the son of a southern peasant, and I told her so. And then she accused me."

His voice trembled and he could not go on.

"Of what did she accuse you, Baba?"

He looked at me piteously, his lower lip trembling. "She said that, because I was a foreigner, I did not want the revolution to come. She even said that I wished to keep the Emperor on the throne for the sake of my salary. When I declared that I would resign immediately, she said it made no difference, for then I would persist in my ways for the sake of my own people. She said our two races could never mingle. She said I was loyal to my own. She had been sweet and gentle, and now suddenly she was cruel and angry with me. She said I had never loved her."

Ah, that was the reason for the change! I understood, for I, too, am a woman. She loved and knew she was not loved, and so she left her home and wandered where she could find shelter. I had not the heart to tell Baba what he did not know—or had forgotten.

"This was because of Gerald?"

He shook his head. "I do not know."

But I knew. Her heart had woken when she saw her son. This child, half-white, she had borne in ignorance of his fate. Where was his place? She knew that if he went to the land of his father, she would be left without love. His place must be in her country, and that she might keep him, she would make a new country for him. Oh, I do not doubt that I am putting it very crudely. She would not have said it so, and perhaps would not even have thought it so. Doubtless she imagined she did all for the sake of her people. She listened to the old arguments, that her people were insulted, the land threatened by foreigners. But I know that all arguments are specious. We do what we do for secret reasons of our own, and this is true in whatever country men and women dwell. She wanted to keep her son. Now I perceive the web she wove about Gerald.

Baba had stopped talking.

"What then, Baba?" I asked.

He sighed and I took up my knitting. He had slipped away. His mind subsided. Yet I could not bear to hear no more. I tried again, as gently as I could.

"How old was Gerald when his mother died?"

Baba spoke with sudden promptness, surprising me so that I dropped my knitting.

"She did not die. She was killed."

"What!"

We sat staring at each other. I saw something terrible now in Baba's eyes, not sorrow, not vagueness. No, I saw fright.

"I warned her," he said. He was trembling, his knees shaking under the thin silk of his robe. "I told her that I could not save her if she persisted. For she became a revolutionist, she became a violent revolutionist—you understand? Not merely a patriot, you understand. She became one of Them."

"Baba—no!"

"Yes, yes! First she became a friend of the wife of

Sun Yat-sen. The two women spent hours together, sometimes in my house. I forbade it at last. I was afraid for myself and for Gerald. I told her that if she must meet with those—traitors—yes, that was the word I used—I said, 'If you must meet with those traitors, Ai-lan, it shall not be in my house, or in the presence of my son.' And she took those two words and threw them back at me as one flings a dagger.

" 'Your son!' "

I heard the Chinese voice as clearly as though she stood in this room. Thousands of miles and years away I heard the words.

"Oh Baba, go on!"

"She went out of my house and I never saw her again."

"She was not dead?"

"No—not then. I went to her brother, my friend, and we searched for her. He was entirely with me, you understand. He begged my forgiveness for having given his sister to me for my wife. He denounced her and disowned her, and he said he would erase her name from the book of family history. It was he who found her at last. But he would not tell me where she was. He said, 'It is better for you not to know.' I knew what he meant. She had joined herself to Them. She was with Them in the South, where they were making the revolution. She and the wife of Sun Yat-sen, they were like sisters."

"Did Gerald never see her again either?"

For all the time Baba was talking, it was of Gerald that I was thinking. I saw him growing up in that great house, alone with his father, but dreaming, I suppose, of his mother. What child does not dream of his mother? When I had first finished college I

taught for a year in an orphanage in New York, a
foundling home for girls. Bed and crib lay side by
side, rooms full of children who had been deserted
and betrayed. By day they played and sometimes
even laughed, but at night I was often waked by the
dreadful sound of their weeping. My room was in
another wing, I had no duty toward them at night,
a nurse was near them. But again and again I was
waked. For when a child moaned in her sleep she
murmured "mother," and the word waked every child
of the twenty or thirty in the room, one and then
another, and they wailed the word aloud. "Mother—
mother—" Their crying pervaded the night air and
woke other rooms of lonely children until the whole
building trembled with the voices of sorrowful children, weeping for mothers they could not remember
or had never known. Who can assuage such grief?
I gave up my job and went away, but I have never
forgotten the weeping children, dreaming of their unknown mothers. The child Gerald, lonely in the house
with his foreign father, takes his place with the weeping children.

"He did see his mother," Baba said, in answer to
my question. "She was very correct about that. She
would not see him secretly, since she had left my
house, but she asked, through her brother, whether
Gerald might come to her."

"And you were willing?"

"Not at first. I did not wish his mind to be con-
taminated. I told Han Yu-ren so. I said she must not
contaminate the child's mind. She continued to be
correct. She said that she would not teach him anything and I should be his teacher. I allowed him
therefore to meet her. She came to Peking in order

that she might see him. They met in her ancestral home."

"Was it for hours or days?" I asked.

"Sometimes for hours, sometimes for days, depending upon what she considered her duties to Them. They always came first."

"Ah, the child must have felt that. Gerald is over-sensitive to people. Even as he could not believe before we were married that I loved him, time and again after our marriage I had to prove to him not only that he was the beloved, but that he was lovable. I resorted to pretended jealousy, as for example when we were invited to the Legation Ball, the last winter we were together. I said, "Gerald, don't dance more than once with anyone but me, will you?"

He could still blush. "Don't be silly," he said.

What he did not know was that I was never jealous. I was sure of him because I was sure of myself. It did not matter how many beautiful foreign girls might be at a diplomatic ball, I was not jealous. Gerald is handsome enough for jealousy, that I acknowledged. But he is mine. I was not afraid even of the lovely modern Chinese girls, slim in their straight long robes. I am glad now to remember that I was not afraid, though it was touching that he was pleased at the suggestion. Beloved that he is, I can see that with all his brilliance and wisdom, he is also sometimes naïve.

"What I did not like," Baba was saying, "was that the child longed to live in his mother's ancestral house. He did not return willingly to me. I suppose that he was given sweets and made much of by servants and lesser relatives. You know how it is."

I did know. Those great old ancestral Chinese families adore their men children. In the men children

is their hope of eternal life. The boys are guarded
and pampered and loved. They are absorbed into the
mighty ocean of love, centuries old. Only the strongest and the most self-sufficient can emerge from such
love into independent beings. I think my dead child
could have been such a one had she been a boy. But
she was a girl. Her name was Ruan. I try not to think
of her. I have seen many children but never one like
her. My firstborn she was, and Gerald was Chinese
enough so that I saw disappointment in his eyes when
he came into the hospital room. She lay in the crook
of my arm, my right arm. How strangely one remembers the small useless details!

"Your daughter, sir," I said to Gerald. I was very
gay and happy in those days, in love with my whole
life, with my husband, my house, the city of Peking,
the country of China.

He sat down beside the bed and he gravely in-
spected the child. I saw he was doing his best to hide
his disappointment.

"She is quite small," he said.

I was angry. "On the contrary, Gerald. She weighs
eight pounds. Also she is intelligent."

"Intelligent," he murmured, staring at the round
sleeping face.

"Yes." I yielded to him nearly always but suddenly
I knew I would never yield to him about my daughter.
She was to be beautiful, strong and intelligent. And
so she was and so she continued to be, until at the age
of five she died.

Oh, let me not think of her death, not upon the
anniversary of my wedding night.

"Baba, you are tired," I said and I rolled up my

knitting. "You must go to bed. We will talk another time."

"I have not finished," he said and did not move. So I waited.

"I have not told you how Gerald's mother was killed," he said.

No, he had not told me. It was a dread death, that I could see. I saw it in his wrinkled eyes staring at the dark window, the pinched whiteness about his nostrils, his tightened lips.

"She was shot," he said. He was trembling again and I could not bear it.

"Baba—don't tell me! Don't think of it."

He went on as though I had not spoken. "In the year 1930, in the city of Nanking, she was seized by order of the secret police of the Nationalist government. She was living alone. She had not accompanied her friend, Madame Sun. She had not left with the others on the Long March. For reasons I never knew she had been told to remain in the city. Perhaps she was a spy. I do not know. But she was taken from her bed one cold morning in early spring, before dawn, and she was forced to walk, just as she was, in her night robes, to the Drum Tower, and there, with her back to the wall, and her eyes not blindfolded, she was shot and killed."

I wanted to ask no other question. But I had to ask. "Baba—how did you know?"

"She had a servant, an old woman. That woman found her way to me. She said that her mistress had told her to find me somehow—" His voice faded to silence.

There was no more to tell. His whole frame seemed to shrink. His eyelids dropped over his staring eyes.

"Come, Baba," I said. "Come with me. You are too weary." And I led him to his room and stayed near until he was in bed and at last asleep. . . .

One more question I wish I had asked. Oh, I wish I had asked Baba if Gerald was ever told the manner of his mother's death. I think he was. Perhaps it is not necessary to ask. The Chinese tell each other everything. Who can keep a secret there? Even if the old woman never told, and if Baba never told, someone would have told. Gerald knows.

Yesterday the answer came to the question I did not ask. The postman brought a magazine under Chinese stamps. There are three of them on the magazine. I had not seen these new Communist stamps before. One is orange, one is purple and one is blue. Each carries the face of a young man. One is a soldier, one is a machinist, one is a peasant. There is no name on the wrapper. It merely says P.O.B. No. 305, Peking, China. But I know Gerald sent it. For when I opened the magazine, I found it was dedicated to a martyr of the revolution. She was shot in Nanking on May the fifteenth, 1930. Her name was Han Ai-lan. She was Gerald's mother. There is a picture of her on the cover. I sit looking at it, here by the window where the light falls clear. The face is calm and austere, a narrow face, the eyes large and lustrous, the hair drawn back from the high forehead, the lips, tenderly cut in youth, perhaps, were stern. I can see Gerald's face emerging from this face. The lines are the same.

So my question, unasked, is answered. Gerald knows everything. I do not doubt now that the old woman bore a message to him from his mother. The mother would have told the son how she died and for what cause.

He did know, he did remember. For it was he who set our wedding day, May the fifteenth. He set the day and did not tell me why, but I know now. He cannot write me a letter, but he has sent me his mother's picture and the story of her life—not her life as wife and mother, but her life as a revolutionist, after he was born. There is no mention of him here. But he wants me to know. He wants me to know and to understand. Oh, beloved, I try, I try.

It grows no easier to live alone, woman without man. I feel a certain hardness in me. I am not as tenderhearted as I was. The daily exercise of love is gone and I fear an atrophy. I wonder how other women live, who have had husbands and have them no more. That I must not say of myself, for Gerald still lives. He is not dead but liveth. I do not read the Scriptures often, not regularly, but now I crave spiritual food and I find it wherever the spirit of man has written its travail. This morning, not a day of resurrection, not the cool Easter dawn, but a summer's day in early June, full of life and burgeoning, the garden forcing itself, the late apple trees in full blossom, the grass new green, I felt my blood running through me, too swift and strong, and my soul cried out for succor. Then I took the small worn leather-bound New Testament which had been my father's, and it opened to these words. "He is not dead but liveth." It is enough. I closed the book and went to my work.

. . . Oh, good hard work that a farm has ever ready —I bless it. I went to the barn and there discovered that my prize cow, Cecily, had in the night presented me with a fine heifer calf. Mother and child are doing well, and Cecily looked at me smugly through the bars of the maternity stall. She is a pink-nosed Guernsey and she is slightly dish-faced, which lends her a saucy air. Her figure is impeccable, by Guernsey standards. She did not rise when she saw me, excusing herself doubtless by her achievement. The calf is exquisite, a fawn, dainty head and good lines of back and rump. Since we are strangers, she stared at me with faint alarm, and her mother licked her cheek for reassurance. All traces of birth were cleaned away. Cecily is a good housekeeper in such matters, and she was complacent. In gratitude I offered her the mash that Matt concocts for such occasions, but she ate it without greed, delicately and as a favor to me.

I came away cheered, not only by the possession of another fine heifer, but by pleasure. Life flows on, whatever the need of the heart. I turned to the garden and fell upon the young weeds, though of all tasks I hate weeding. The seeds are up, however, and the race is on. I worked hard all day, stopping only to make luncheon for Baba and me at noon. Matt takes his lunch on the outdoor terrace upon such a day as this, and Rennie is in the last lap of his school year and does not come home at midday. He goes to college in the autumn and what that means I do not know. I fear my loneliness but I must not feed upon him. Baba and I will live here together, like two old folk. . . .

Ah, but I am not old. Tonight when the young moon rose, I could not go to bed. Rennie is away this evening. He is in love, I think. He put on his best dark-blue suit, a white shirt and a crimson tie. He had even polished his Sunday shoes. I do not know who she is. I must wait.

Baba went to bed early. He likes to be under cover, as he puts it, by half-past eight. But it is only the beginning of night then, and I came to the narrow terrace that faces the moon, and lay down on the long chair. The air is chill, though it is June, and I wrapped myself in my white shawl and let myself dream of the beloved. I will not let love die, not while he lives, and so I feed on dreams. If the beloved is dead, one must not dream. But I am no true widow. My beloved liveth.

Therefore my mind floats over land and sea to the city which is his, and like a ghost I creep through the streets, and into the gate where he lives. This I have done again and again in the years we have been parted. They are not many years, actually—only five —and there is nothing eternal about our separation. At any moment he may decide to come here to me. If he does, I will not ask a question. I will not ask why did you, or how could you? I will open my arms and receive him. If we live to be old together yet will I never ask him the question that broods in my heart. It is enough that he returns.

There hangs the moon! Upon a summer night in Peking we sit in the east courtyard. Our house belonged once to a Manchu prince, not a high prince, but a lowly one, a younger brother. It is not large enough for a palace, but those who lived in it loved it well enough to add beauty here and there. Thus the gates between the courts are moon-shaped, framed in tiles set in lacelike patterns. A lotus pool lies in the east court, and a cluster of bamboos hides the wall. The street is on the other side of the house, and the court is quiet. Moreover, the east court leads into our bedroom, Gerald's and mine. The huge Chinese bed stands against the inner wall. At first, as a bride, I complained about the bed. It is too hard, I said, a wooden frame and a bottom of woven rattan to sleep upon. I liked the pink satin bed curtains caught back by silver hooks, but I did not like the mattress. Gerald laughed at me and said that I wanted the beauty and not the hardness of Chinese life. And I said why should we sleep on wood and rattan when we could have a spring mattress, and is that a sin? Not sin, he said, but inconsistency. We should be one thing or the other, he said. And this I refused to concede, for why not have the best of both, I said, and so when he went to Tientsin to order supplies for the college year, he brought back an American spring mattress. And it was a game between us that I should pretend to force him to admit its comfort while he pretended to like the old hard Chinese bed bottom. We laughed a great deal in those days, Gerald and I. I do not remember that he laughed with anyone else, not with his pupils or with Rennie or with Baba, but only with me. He was to that degree not like his Chinese friends, for Chinese laugh easily and gaily. But Gerald is grave. He can even be somber. At such times he is always silent. Nothing I could say would make him speak. Only love could bring him back to me, warm physical love, informed by heart and mind. Sitting there alone on the terrace, I stretched out my arms to him across the sea.

Rennie came home at midnight and found me still on the terrace. "You haven't been waiting for me, I hope, Mom?" he said.

Yes, suddenly he is getting to be an American. The stately name of Mother, upon which his father always insisted, has become Mom. I say nothing. What is the use of keeping alive the shadow of his father when the substance is far from here?

"No," I said, "I was just thinking about your father and wondering what he is doing tonight—working, probably."

So much of the substance I mentioned.

Rennie did not answer. Instead, rather ostentatiously, he lit a cigarette. I know that he smokes, and he knows that I know, but it is the first time he has done so before me.

"Give me one, will you?" I said.

He looked surprised enough to amuse me and held out the pack. "I didn't know you smoked," he said and lit my cigarette.

"I don't," I retorted. "But you seem to enjoy it, and why not I?"

He was embarrassed and I fear the pleasure went out of his cigarette. Perhaps it is necessary for the young to have something to defy. I suspect they hate this modern permissiveness. There is nothing in it to set their teeth against. At any rate, Rennie soon put out his cigarette, but I smoked mine to the end.

"Not much to it," I said. "I'd thought there was more."

"You have to inhale."

"When I have time I will."

The moon was sailing high overhead, a sphere of white gold in a pale starless sky. Rennie stretched himself in the other long chair and locked his hands behind his head. I heard him sigh.

"How old were you when you were married, Mom?"

This was his question.

"I was twenty-three. I had just graduated from college the year before."

"Gee, that was old."

"It didn't seem so," I said. "Your father and I were engaged for a year."

"Why didn't you get married before?"

How much does one reveal to a child? Rennie's profile in the moonlight was not a child's. He has grown three and a half inches this year. He is already as tall as Gerald. The bones of his face are hardening and the lines are strengthening. If these are the outward signs of manhood, there must be inward changes, too.

"Your father was afraid I might not like China. More than that, he wanted to be sure that I could love what was Chinese in him. Until he was sure, he would not marry me. It took time. He doesn't give himself all at once."

This our son pondered.

"What is Chinese in him?" he asked at last.

"Don't you know?" It was a parry. I did not know how to answer.

"No. I can't even remember him clearly."

"Why, Rennie, you were twelve when we left."

"I know—I should remember. I don't know why I can't."

He does not want to remember his father—that is why. But I cannot tell him so. It would be accusation and I must not accuse him. Let me seize this opportunity to help him remember.

"You know how he looks."

"He really looks Chinese," Rennie said unwillingly.

"Then you do remember," I said. "Yes, he looks

Chinese until he is with Chinese and then he looks American."

"If he were here he'd look Chinese all right."

"What of it? The Chinese are very handsome, especially northern Chinese, where your grandparents lived. Do you remember your granduncle Han Yu-ren?"

"No."

Well, perhaps not. We did not see Han Yu-ren again. He was a collaborator with the Japanese and when Peking was returned he had disappeared. Rennie knows that much.

"I hope you will never think of your granduncle as a traitor," I said. "I am sure that he believed he was doing what was best. Perhaps Peking would have been destroyed had it not been for him. I can imagine that in times of war, when the enemy is within the gates, many a true patriot yields for the moment that he may preserve the eternal possession of his country. China has been saved many times by such patriots. Think of the Mongol conquerors, think of the Manchus! Men like Han Yu-ren seemed to yield to them, too. But the conquerors came and went and China remained. Remember always that Peking is not to be destroyed."

Rennie said nothing to this. He listened, as the young do listen, in silence, and it is not known how much they comprehend until one sees how they live in after years. I thought of his grandmother, Gerald's mother. Should I tell him? No, not yet. But I shall keep her picture and the commemorative magazine and the time will come.

"Is my father more Chinese inside or more American?" This Rennie asked, while he stared at the moon.

I answered as truthfully as I could. "I shall be hard

put to it to say. I've asked myself that question. I think that when he is Chinese he is very Chinese. There are other times when he is very American."

"For example?"

Rennie has the precise mind of a scientist. How can I answer him? How can I speak of the hours when Gerald and I were man and woman? For it was when we were alone, husband and wife, that Gerald was American. That surely was his true self. Then he put aside the curtains of tradition and habit and no strangeness came between us.

"He is really very Chinese when it comes to family," I said. "He treats you as a Chinese father does his son, gently but with an inexorable loving firmness. He never lets you forget that you are not only his son but you are the grandson, the great-grandson, a thousand times over, of many men before you. The generations are always with you—aren't they?"

"Yes," Rennie said unwillingly. Then he added, after a moment, "But I have other ancestors—yours, Mom—and maybe I'm more like them."

"It may be that you are."

I knew that he had not reached the real meaning of all this talk. What can one do with the young except wait? Soon he began again.

"Mom, do you think my being part Chinese will keep a girl from liking me?"

"An American girl?"

"Of course."

So it is of course!

"Certainly not," I said. "It would be much more likely that a Chinese girl wouldn't like the American in you."

"I couldn't fall for a Chinese girl."

"You might. They're very beautiful, many of them."

"I shan't go back to China," he told me.

"You might go back some day to see your father, if he doesn't come here to us."

"Will he come here, do you think?"

This, this was the moment to tell him about the letter locked in my box upstairs. Sooner or later he will have to be told. I am afraid to tell him. He is too young to understand, too ignorant to have mercy.

"I hope he will come. Let's both hope. And who's the girl, Rennie?"

For of course there is a girl. All the talk has simply been leading up to it. I was suddenly tired.

He sat up surprised. "Mom, how did you know?"

"Oh, I know," I said, trying to laugh. "I really know more than you think I do."

He lay back to stare again at the moon.

"It's nothing to talk about—not yet, I guess. She's the girl in that green and white house down the road. Summer people."

I knew people had moved into the house, but I have been too busy to call on them. Sometimes I call on our summer neighbors and sometimes I do not. Now of course I must go.

"What's her name?"

"Allegra."

"A fanciful name!"

"It's pretty, though, don't you think?"

"Perhaps."

"The last name is Woods," he went on.

"What does the father do?"

"Business of some sort in New York. He isn't here much. Allegra's here with her mother."

"How did you happen to meet?"

"She was walking down the road one day, toward Moore's Falls, and I happened along and she asked where she was."

"You must bring her to see me, if you really like her," I said. All the warnings were quivering inside me. My son is in danger. The hour I had foreseen since the day he was laid in my arms, new born, has now come. A girl has looked at him. He has looked at the girl. What girl is this?

"It's getting cold," I said. "We must go inside and shut the doors."

I hope the friendship will not move too quickly into something else. Rennie brought Allegra here today. They have been meeting every day, I think. It is so easy here in the valley. The long summer days begin early and end late. Rennie works hard with Matt, cleaning the sugar bush on fine days and packing maple sugar or bottling syrup, while I tend house and garden and the barn. Yet there are hours after sunset and before bedtime. I cannot ask him always where he goes and when he will come back. He wants now to be free.

Today, when I had cleared away our supper, he went out and I saw him striding down the road with purpose. In less than an hour he was back, bringing the girl with him.

"Mother," he said, now very formal. "This is Allegra Woods."

I was doing the mending in the living room and the lamp was lit, and Baba was sitting in peaceful silence in the brown leather armchair, his feet, in velvet Chinese shoes, on the hassock. Of course he was wearing his crimson silk Chinese robe. I had helped him wash his hair and his beard today and they were snow white.

"How do you do, Allegra," I said, not getting up. But I took my spectacles off by habit, since it is not good Chinese manners to greet a stranger, or a friend, in spectacles.

The young girl made a graceful movement toward me, not quite a bow nor yet a courtsey. Then she put out a slim hand.

"How do you do, Mrs. MacLeod."

"This is Rennie's grandfather," I said, looking toward Baba.

For some reason of his own Baba decided to be difficult. Instead of greeting Allegra he said in Chinese, very clearly, "Who is this female?"

Rennie flushed. He pretends he has forgotten all his Chinese but when he wishes he remembers it perfectly. He spoke in sharp English. "Grandfather, this is my friend Allegra Woods. Mother wanted to meet her."

Baba stared at Rennie, nodding his head like an old Mandarin, and would not say a word to her. Nor would he look at Allegra.

"She should be at home with her parents," he said in Chinese.

I laughed. "Allegra, you mustn't mind him. He lived in China for so many years he has forgotten he is an American."

Her blue eyes grew wide. "In China? Rennie didn't tell me."

Then Rennie has not told her everything. I must be careful not to tell too much.

"Yes," I said cheerfully. "We all lived there. Rennie's father is still there. As a matter of fact, Rennie was born in Peking."

73

"Really?"

"Very really."

"But I thought China was communist?"

"Just now, yes."

"Then how can his father—"

"He is the president of a great college and he feels it his duty to stay with his students."

"I see."

But she didn't see, that I knew. She looked thoughtfully at Rennie, her eyes big and blue.

"Get some ice cream, Rennie," I said. "There's plenty in the freezer."

"Come along, Allegra." He seized her hand.

This is the beginning. I do not know the end.

We live in a narrow valley. One word can start a forest fire of gossip—one word, for example, like Communist. Or even a word, say, like China . . .

"Did you have to tell her everything at once?" Rennie groaned that night when he came home.

"I did not tell her everything," I said.

Baba had gone to bed, but I had waited, knowing that he must accuse me.

"She said now she knew why I seemed queer," Rennie said and choked.

I longed to put my arms about him but he would have hated it. Better to speak the truth and speak it whole.

"You will have to accept yourself," I said. "You are partly Chinese, one fourth by blood but more, perhaps, in tastes and inclinations. We shall have to see. One thing I know. You will never be happy until you are proud of all that you are—not just of a part. You have a noble inheritance, but it is on both sides of the globe."

I did not look at him. I kissed his cheek and went away. The Allegras of this world are not for him, but he will have to find it out for himself. Then when the pain is over he will discover a woman who is his, and whose he can be. Whether she is Chinese, or American, who knows or cares?

What, I wonder, made me know Gerald was mine? I was, it seems to me now, a very ordinary girl. There had been nothing enlarging in my childhood. Even my mother was a limiting influence. She had no large emotions, no world feelings. The church to which we went taught me nothing of the much-talked-of and seldom practiced brotherhood. My father was skeptic, but he was not a preacher even of his own ideas.

I remember that spring day in my senior year at Radcliffe. I was hurrying to my class in philosophy, my arm full of books, for I was a studious girl, but in those days we were not ashamed of it. Nowadays, it seems, if I am to judge by what Rennie tells me, boys do not like studious girls. Allegra, for example, has a pretty way of seeming stupid, although I do not know whether she is. But I did not think of such pretense. I was late to class that spring day, and much distracted by the beauty of the season and the warmth of the sunshine, while I tried to keep in my head the ponderous meanings of Kant's categorical imperative. And at that predestined moment I saw Gerald run with his striking grace down the steps of the hall I was about to enter. I shall remember forever, though my eyes, one day, be blind with age, the glint of the sun on his black hair, the lively glance of his black eyes, and the clear smoothness of his cream skin.

The Chinese have some magic in the structure of

their skin and even a little of the blood seems to purify the flesh. Rennie has the same faultlessness of skin. I do not wonder that Allegra likes to dance with her cheek against his as I saw them doing last Saturday night in our small community center. So too do I love to dance, cheek to cheek, with Gerald. We did not speak that day on the steps, but we looked full into one another's eyes, and instantly I made up my mind forever. I would learn what his name was and tell him he was mine.

It did not happen in a day or a week but it did in a month. For I kept looking at him because he was handsome, and then because he was the most beautiful man I had ever seen. Soon I was speaking to him, managing to walk out the door of a classroom when he did. And he was so shy that I had to keep on walking beside him down the corridor lest he leave me, and so to the front gate of the building and into the street. He could not shake me off. And then, making a pretext of his being foreign and perhaps without friends, I asked him one day to meet my mother, and so it all began. I was in love.

And yet when he let me know at last—oh what a long time it was before he let me know, two months, three months, four months—I thought he would never tell me. Even when he began to tell me, he hesitated, he delayed.

"Go on, go on," I said, laughing with joy.

"I don't know whether you can consider me as a friend—" He wet his dry lips.

"I can and I do," I said.

After we were married, I asked him why he stammered so much that day, for it was day, high noon, and we were sitting on a bench beside the Charles

River, our books piled on the ground at our feet. He said, stammering again, though by then we were in our bedroom by the east court of the Peking house, and we had been happy together that night and were about to sleep, "The—the fact is, I never thought I'd be—be in love, you know—with an American girl."

"Didn't you, now," I teased. "And whom would you be marrying please, if not me?"

And he said soberly, "I had always supposed I would marry a Chinese. My uncle told me it was my mother's wish."

That is what he said, long ago, when his mother was nothing to me except a dead woman, and what she said meant nothing, either. I had even forgotten that midnight, until now, when Allegra brings it out of my memory.

I keep looking at the picture of Gerald's mother. I have put it away again and again. Each time I say forever, until or unless some day I must show it to Rennie, and then her face appears in my mind and I am restless until I see her with my eyes. So tonight I have taken her picture out of the locked drawer of my desk, and it lies here before me, the same calm unchanging face. It is not cold. The surface only is cold. Behind the calm steadfast eyes of a Chinese woman I feel a powerful warmth. We might have been friends, she and I, unless she had decided first that I was her enemy. She would have decided, not I. I was never deceived by Chinese women, not even by the flowerlike lovely girls. They are the strongest women in the world. Seeming always to yield, they never yield. Their men are weak beside them. Whence comes this female strength? It is the strength that centuries have given them, the strength of the unwanted. It was always the sons who were welcomed at birth. It was always the sons who were given privilege and protection and pampering love. And the daughter had to accept this, generation after generation, and to bear it in silence. She learned to think first of herself—to protect herself in secret, to steal what she was not given, to lie lest the truth bring her harm, to use deceit as a shield and a cover for her own ends, those ends her own safety and her own pleasure when she was only a female, but how magnificent in sacrifice if she were a great woman, as Gerald's mother was.

I have put the picture into the drawer again and locked it fast. But it haunts me. Today, which is Saturday, Baba and I being at lunch together alone, since Rennie is off fishing, or so he told me, I could not refrain from speaking again of her.

"Baba, you remember we were speaking of Gerald's mother?"

"Were we?"

He was eating neatly with chopsticks, a habit which he assumes whenever I cook rice, which is often, because he accepts it with appetite when he will take nothing else.

"Yes, we were," I said, "and I want to talk more about her."

He put down his chopsticks. "What is it you wish to know?"

"I have a picture of her upstairs."

He turned quite pale. "How is it you have it?"

"It is in a magazine."

I could not tell him Gerald had sent it.

"Fetch it," he said.

I ran upstairs and brought it down and placed it

before him. He put on his spectacles and looked at it carefully. "Ye-es," he said slowly, "ye-es, I can recognize her. But it is not as she used to look."

"How did she look?"

He knitted his white eyebrows, thinking. "When I lifted her wedding veil, I thought her nearly beautiful."

"Yes, Baba?" This was because he paused so long.

"Afterwards I was not sure. She could make her face quite strange to me."

"Why did she?"

"I did not ask. We were never close enough for questions."

I could not deny my impulse. "But you had a child together."

A faded pink crept into his cheeks. "Well, yes."

"You won't deny Gerald, I hope?" I had to laugh at him a little.

"No—oh, no. But you see—"

"I don't, Baba."

"A child doesn't have much to do with one—you know. I mean—well, such things happen."

"For men—not for women."

"I daresay."

He cleared his throat. "At any rate, after Gerald was born, there was no more of that sort of thing."

"Your wish?"

"No—hers."

"How well you remember, Baba!"

"I forget very much," he said vaguely.

He took up his chopsticks again and began to eat. He remembers but he no longer feels. And I wonder if by some strange chance that Chinese woman did love him long ago, and because he did not love her,

79

she took what she had, the child, and made the child her own. Who can tell me now? But the child was Gerald.

Tonight the moon is full upon the mountains and the shadows in the valley are black. Our valley is wide, and the terrace looks westward upon it. The graveled road is silvered and I see two figures walking slowly at the far end into the trees, their arms entwined. I know they are Rennie and Allegra.

It is a misfortune that these two met in the spring. It is not so easy to fall in love in winter. Winter is for married love in firelit evenings and a house enclosed in snow. The snow fell deep in Peking and the drifts against the gate were as good as any lock. The Chinese admire the beauty of snow, their painters love the white of late snow against the pink of peach blossoms or the red of berries on the Indian bamboo, but they do not like to go out in snow, their shoes being of cloth or velvet, and so Gerald and I had no visitors on snowy nights. Even the old watchman stayed prudently in his little room by the gate, and we were safely alone. We heaped the brazier with coals and we put out the candles and sat by the glow of the fire. That was the time for love, the long night stretching ahead in hours of endless happiness.

Here in Vermont, too, the snow makes me prisoner, but not of love. I sit by the fire alone and Rennie studies his books in his own room. Now it is summer and I am still alone, for Rennie is with Allegra. They have reached the end of the road. They have walked out of the moonlight into the shadows beneath the maple trees. I cannot see them. It is not the first evening. A change began with the new moon this month.

I knew it because I felt it in Rennie. He was silent and hurried, not by work or necessity but because of haste and urgency in himself. He came and went without speaking and if he saw me looking at him he knew I asked why he was changed, and he turned his head away and did not answer.

Last night when he came in I could bear it no longer, for whom have I if Rennie leaves me? I had stayed until long past midnight upon the terrace, so late that the wind was cool and I wrapped my red wool scarf about me. Then I saw Rennie springing up the hill. He looked like a man in the night, so tall and strong and powerful. Something has made him a man. He came near and saw me and he did not come to the terrace, but went instead to the door of the kitchen.

"Rennie!"

At the sound of my voice he paused, his hand on the latch.

"Yes?"

"Come here, please."

He came, not unwillingly, even quietly and calmly.

"You're late," he said.

"I have waited for you."

His voice is a man's voice now. "You mustn't wait for me—not any more."

"I cannot sleep when I do not know where you are," I said.

"You will have to learn to sleep, not knowing."

He said this coolly and I was suddenly angry because I knew he was right. And being angry I could not keep from speaking the truth.

"I know you are with Allegra every evening and I don't like her."

It is the first time I have spoken my growing dislike for this girl whom Rennie is beginning to love. Beginning? I do not know how deeply he has gone into love. I do not know what he thinks about love. If Gerald were here, as he should be, to help me with our son, I could talk with him and heed his advice. But would he speak to Rennie? My neighbor, Mrs. Landes, a grandmother, says that fathers cannot "speak" to their sons. She says that her own husband would never "speak" to the boys. They are grown now and married, but he did not speak, and she could not speak.

"But why?" I asked her.

"Because it would make me feel naked before my own boys," she said downrightly.

Her boys have married good valley women. Perhaps in their plain inarticulate lives it is better not to speak. Words may be too much for the simple acts of physical union. I do not know. But I have known the fullness of love, an achievement absolute in height and depth, and I wish for my son a like joy.

"Sit down, Rennie," I said. "It is late, but not too late for what I want to say." He sat down on the low wall of the terrace, his back to the rising moon so that his face was in shadow and mine in the light. And I went on:

"It is not that I disapprove of Allegra for her own sake. She is like many other girls, pretty and sweet and shallow. She will make some man quite happy, a man who does not need much, a man who is like most men, requiring little from anyone, a joiner of clubs, a hail-fellow-well-met sort of man, with plenty of easy friends, not a reader of books, a man who likes gay music, if he likes any, a man who goes to the movies on Saturday nights and enjoys cowboys. He will be happy with Allegra and she with him, and they will do very well together, for the heart of each has the measure of a cup and no more, and so they fulfill one another. But you, Rennie, will not be satisfied with no more than a cup of love. You need a fountain, living and eternal. You must find a deep woman, my son, a woman with an overflowing heart. When you find her, believe me, I shall never lie awake again, however late you come home. I shall be at rest."

"You don't know Allegra," he said.

"A mother always knows the girl her son loves."

I had never said such a thing before, nor even thought it, but it came to me now, a truth welling through me from the generations of women from whom I have sprung.

"Allegra says you are jealous," Rennie retorted.

"That is because she knows she is not the one you should love, and she knows that I know it, too."

We were on the edge of a great bitterness, my son and I, and I drew back from the abyss. I did not want to hear him speak words which would dash us over the precipice together. I did not want to hear him say that he had better go away because I did not understand him. I summoned Gerald to my aid and I tried to speak calmly.

"I suppose the reason I long so much for you to love one who can truly love you is because your father and I have been utterly happy together. From the moment I saw him I knew him for mine. I had never loved another man, nor had he loved a woman before me. It is old-fashioned, I know. It is quite the thing now, I hear, to say that one must experiment in love and that it does not matter how many people one experiments with before the final one is found. Perhaps that is true for the shallow-hearted. But it is not true for the deep in heart. Your father and I are among those few. It made our love complete when we knew that what we gave each to the other was new and never given before. I assure you it did."

How glad I am now that I have never shown Rennie the letter I have locked in my desk upstairs! For whatever the letter means, I know that what I say is true. I know that Gerald still loves only me. But Rennie could not know. It will be a long time before he can know, and he will never know if he does not find his mate.

"It's strange then that my father does not even write to you," he said cruelly.

"Not strange," I replied. "He knows that I know he loves me, and he knows I love him, unchangingly. There is some reason why he cannot write, a reason that has nothing to do with you and me. There are many such reasons that separate people in the world now. We must not allow them to destroy love. We must wait, still loving."

I was teaching myself as well as Rennie, but I am not sure he knew it. One can only know a little when one is young. I do wonder that I could know, when I myself was young, that Gerald was the beloved the moment I saw him. It was not wisdom, for I had no wisdom then and not much now.

Rennie got up and came to me and kissed my cheek. "You needn't worry, Mom," he said. "And you're wrong about Allegra. She's all right. Anyway, I'm not my father and she is not you, and we have to live our own lives."

To this there could be no reply, and he went upstairs. He reminds me twenty times a day without knowing it of these two facts, that he is not his father and that he has to live his own life. I went upstairs after his window was dark, and that night I slept fitfully. I dreamed that I searched everywhere through the house in Peking and could not find Gerald. He had gone. I woke then in terror, and knew my own house safely about me here in Vermont, but how lonely!

Tonight when Rennie came out of the shadows, I saw him stand for a long last moment with Allegra in his arms. It was so late they did not care, for who was there to see them? The people in our valley go to bed early. He stood, my tall son, with his arms clasped about the slender girl, and her face was lifted to his. They kissed the long passionate kiss of first love and then, wrapped in each other's arms, they walked slowly up the moonlit road to her house. I lost him at the gate, for he took her to the door and it was a full quarter of an hour before he came to the gate again alone. Then he sauntered up the road, his hands in his pockets. I was on the terrace as usual when he reached the house. I was determined to let him see that I was not comforted, nor was my anxiety assuaged. Allegra tonight was to me what she had been on the other night. He saw me there on the long chair, and this time he called to me.

"Good night, Mom!"

"Good night, my son," I said.

I heard him clatter up the backstairs from the kitchen to his room. My father put those stairs in for the hired man, so that the fellow could come and go without disturbing the family. And this summer Rennie moved from the room next to mine, where he has lived since we came home, announcing that he would take the room over the kitchen. It is a pleasant room, low-ceiled but large, and it has a separate bath, my father having been fastidious. "A man who bathes only on Saturday night needs a bathroom for himself alone," he said.

I know of course why Rennie wants that room. It is so that he can come and go without passing my door. I know ruefully that he has the right to come and go now without telling me. And if Allegra were the girl I dream of for him, I would not care. But Allegra! Yet no mother can save her son. She can only watch and wait and wring her hands. I wonder if he understood when I spoke of deep-hearted love? I am sure he does not. And now I am sorry for Allegra, too, for if this goes on he will make demands on her far beyond what she is able to give. His passion will mightily exceed hers, and she will be made miserable because she knows she is not enough for him. So thinking, I perceive that it is Allegra I pity and I see that she must be protected, too, from Rennie. She is a woman, however small her heart, and it is wrong for her to be unhappy. I am for women even against my son. I had not thought of it so before. Deeper than motherhood is womanhood.

This discovery, which I have made only now as I write, is bewildering. I do not know what I shall do with it. Yet I feel suddenly eased. I am not thinking of Rennie alone. What I am thinking has to do with men and women. It is chance, beatific and blessed, that made Gerald and me well mated. Had not my father left the money in his will to send me to college, specifying Radcliffe because he had no son to send to

Harvard, I might have chosen someone as Rennie has. One takes what one finds at this age. I must save Rennie as my father saved me, but Allegra must be saved, too.

It is long past midnight. I am too tired to think clearly about this new responsibility. Morning will bring light.

Today Rennie is full of joy. He thinks he has clarified his relationship to me. He is free, he thinks, and he came downstairs this morning all life and cheer, his beautiful face aglow, his eyes shining with love. He kissed me briskly on the cheek, careful now never to touch my lips, and sat down at the table to eat a breakfast to match the day.

"I must begin cleaning the brush from the high sugar bush," he said, his voice loud and clear. "Matt can help me when he has done the barn. The manure should go on the far pasture."

"I suppose so," I said.

He was off then, very busy—and I washed the dishes and tended the house. Rennie thinks I should have a dishwasher but I will not. I like the quiet reflective moments after a meal, my hands in the hot soapy water and the view from the kitchen window before my eyes. Then, too, I love my dishes. Some I brought with me from the house in Peking, and the rest are my mother's and ones that I used as a child. I do not understand women who complain about their houses and their children and their husbands. This is our dear daily work. And I do not like new things. It takes time to become acquainted with possessions, and they should not change. Whenever a dish is lost or broken, something of life goes with it. This morning I used for porringers the blue Chinese bowls lined with yellow porcelain. Alas, when I washed mine, it slipped from my fingers and fell against the sink and broke into pieces. I could not keep the tears from rushing to my eyes. Nor could I bear to throw the bits of lovely pottery into the garbage pail. I carried them outside and buried them under the old apple tree by the front door.

When I came back into the kitchen Baba was there, waiting to be fed. He is growing very old now, and childish. I tucked the napkin in his collar but he would not lift his hand to his spoon, and I fed him. He ate then quite patiently, in silence, his eyes fixed vaguely on the window. He will wear only his Chinese robes these days, and when he speaks it is nearly always in Chinese.

"I go back to my bed," he said when the dish was empty.

"Sit on the terrace a while in the sun," I suggested.

He shook his head and I had to coax him. "Do you not remember how the grandfathers in Peking always sit against the walls of the houses where the sun shines? They do not get out of bed and eat and go back to bed again. They like the sun, and the air is warm today and without wind."

He rose obediently after this and I wrapped a scarf about his neck and led him by the hand to the terrace and sat him down on the bench against the wall. He sat there without moving, his eyes closed as though he slept, and I forgot him. At noon, ashamed, I hurried out to find him still there, panting somewhat with the heat, his cheeks pink, and his blue eyes open in reproach.

"Shall I go to bed now?" he inquired.

"Indeed you shall," I said, "after you have had some tea and a boiled egg with your rice."

He ate without demur, relishing the Chinese tea, and I took him up to bed, and pulled the shades and left him fast asleep. The sun and air did him good, but how could I forget him? How selfish to let my mind dwell only upon my son!

Yet the hours of thought while I tended my house have cleared my mind. There is no better time to think and ponder than in the hours when a woman sweeps and dusts and makes beds. The physical activity sends blood coursing through her frame and the brain awakes. Yes, I shall go to see Allegra's mother. I do not know how much she can comprehend of what I wish to say. And when I come back I shall tell Rennie what I did. I will have no secrets. And I shall maintain that it is my right to be free to act—if his, then mine.

Mrs. Woods was sitting on the porch of her house when I opened the gate. The house is a pleasant one, painted white and the shutters green, a conventional house even to the flower beds and the walk between them. She was sewing needlepoint, an art my mother tried to teach me, but I never cared for it and forgot what I was taught.

Mrs. Woods rose when I came to the steps. She is a plump, middle-aged woman, not fat, a round friendly face, curled hair, the sort of woman to be seen on any porch anywhere, a good woman, somewhat timid, as American women often are, and I do not know why they are. Chinese women may be shy or pretend they are, and it is nine-tenths pretense, because they think women should be shy, or because men like them shy, but they are never timid.

"Come in," Mrs. Woods said, seeming flustered.

"I am Mrs. Gerald MacLeod," I said, "and I live up the road."

"I know your boy Rennie," she said. "Come along in. We'd best sit inside, I think, because the mites are bad today. I was just about to move."

We went inside a narrow hall with a red carpet, the straight stairs leading to the second floor. To the right was a neat dining room and to the left a largish living room, furnished as most living rooms are. It was pleasant and comfortable. There were a few magazines on the table beside the couch, but no books. How could Rennie live in a house without books?

"Take that chair," Mrs. Woods said. "It's my husband's, and so it's the most comfortable."

There was suddenly a mild twinkle in her gray eyes that I liked. I sat down and came to the point at once.

"I'm sure you know that Rennie and Allegra are going together. I want to know what you think about it. They're so young, and there aren't any other young people very near."

Her round face grew concerned. She has a round little mouth and round eyes and her nose turns up enough to show her two round nostrils. It is a sweet childish face. She must have been a pretty baby. Allegra is much prettier. The father, perhaps, has straightened the lines of her face. But she has her mother's curved figure, rounded hips and full breasts, enchanting now but not forever. Mrs. Woods is tightly corseted. These foolish details swarmed in my mind while I waited for her to speak.

"They are young," she agreed. "Mr. Woods and I

have been worried some. Of course we want Allegra to feel free. But she's only a senior in high school next year. We live in Passaic, New Jersey. The schools are good there. We wouldn't want Allegra to think she didn't want to finish high school."

"Heavens, no," I said in horror. "And Rennie will have to go to college—it's Harvard, where his father and grandfather went—and after that he will have still more years somewhere, perhaps in Europe, or perhaps in China, where his father is."

Real horror broke over my neighbor's face. "China? Nobody can go there, can they?"

"Not now," I said, "but hopefully Rennie may join his father there some day, when the world is better."

"Is his father—a Chinese?" Mrs. Woods spoke the word apologetically.

"No," I said, "at least, not altogether, or my name wouldn't be MacLeod. His father, Rennie's grandfather, is American. He lives with us. He's old—and he's not well. He never leaves home."

I had said so much that she waited for me to say more, and I went on. "My husband is president of a great university in Peking. We had hoped that he could join us here, but he feels it his duty to stay by his work."

"Isn't China communist?" Her voice was vaguely reproachful.

"Yes," I said, "and my husband is not communist, I can assure you. But he still feels he must stay by his work and do it the best he can." Then the truth forced itself from me. "You see, his mother was Chinese—and so—"

"She was?" Mrs. Wood's voice was an exclamation.

"Then that's why Rennie—we thought maybe he had Indian blood."

"Didn't Rennie tell Allegra?"

"No, no, I'm sure he didn't. Allegra tells me everything. I know she'd have told me."

"Then I am glad I told. It is better for you to know before they fall too much in love."

"I should say so."

Her mind was busy in her face. She flushed with thought, she bit her small full lips, she forgot me. Her plump small hands were clenched together on her lap. Suddenly she looked up and her eyes met mine.

"You poor thing," she said. "It's dreadful for you, isn't it?"

"What—Rennie?"

"The whole business—marrying somebody way off— a Chinese!"

"My husband is American," I said. "His father registered his birth at the American Embassy in Peking. Rennie was registered there, too."

"Still and all—it's different, somehow."

"I've been completely happy," I said. "So happy that I must make sure Rennie will be happy, too. I couldn't let him marry a girl who merely tolerated his being partly Chinese. She must be glad of it. She must be proud of it. She must understand that he is the richer for it, as a man and a person—yes, even as an American."

She could not follow me. She tried, bless her, for somehow I could not keep from liking her more and more. She is simple and honest. I hope she will continue as my friend, whatever happens. I would like to know someone like her intimately, so that we could talk as woman to woman. I miss a good friend. Matt's wife is good, but she is ignorant and besides she and Matt quarrel over some past grief which neither tells me. They live alone on the mountainside opposite ours, their children gone now, and they quarrel constantly. Matt groans sometimes on a gray morning, "Oh, that woman has been the death of me these forty years!" And when I take a lettuce to Mrs. Matt she tells me of Matt's wickedness and how he won't shave but once a week however she tells him, and she declares that he's been torture these forty years. She has no capacity for friendship. But Mrs. Woods is a happy wife and mother. I can see that. It is not her fault that her heart holds only a cupful.

And it is her fortune that her husband needs no more. For he came in after a while, a thin, bald man, his eyes very blue. This is his vacation, he told me. He works in an accountant's office in Passaic and he has two weeks a year free to do what he likes. I suddenly pitied him. Two weeks!

"Do you enjoy your work, Mr. Woods?" I asked. This was after we had been introduced, and he told me what he did, and how good it was just to loaf.

"I like my job, but I'm glad not to work," he said.

"Though there's plenty of work to be done about the place," his wife said in reproach. But she spoke gently and even lovingly, and he smiled at her. He was not afraid of her, and she would not urge him. It was an amicable marriage between equals, and therefore pleasant to contemplate. They would understand, to the extent of a cupful, what I mean when I talk about happiness.

"I am your neighbor, Mr. Woods, and frankly I

came to see you and Mrs. Woods about my son and your daughter. They are both so young," I said.

He was instantly embarrassed as only good American men can be embarrassed when anyone mentions male and female together in the presence of their wives or mothers or middle-aged women. For all their adolescent interest in physical sex, they are singularly pure and unsophisticated. They scatter their seed around the earth these days, begetting children in Europe and Asia as innocently and irresponsibly as young tomcats in spring. They pause to mate, and then wander on.

"Mrs. MacLeod tells me her husband is Chinese," Mrs. Woods said significantly.

"No, no," I cried. "I said that he is American, an American citizen, although his mother was Chinese. She was a lady of high birth, her family one of the great families of Peking. She is dead now."

"No kidding," Mr. Wood exclaimed in a low voice. "Well, now! I don't know as I ever heard of anyone mixed like that."

He was bewildered. It was obvious that he was shocked and at the same time was too kind to show it. He did not want to hurt me. He was sorry for me, and couldn't put it into words. He looked at his wife helplessly. They were both sweet people and I began to love them, knowing while I did so that they could not understand me now and would never understand me. Gerald had been right to stay in Peking.

But I had Rennie to think of and I got up. "Thank you both," I said as cheerfully as I could. "Please don't worry. Rennie will be going off to college soon, and young people forget easily. I don't think it has gone very deep. As for Allegra, she is so pretty that she must have a lot of boy friends."

They grasped at the suggestion. "She is very popular," Mrs. Woods said proudly.

"In fact," Mr. Woods said, "she was voted the most popular girl in high school last summer."

"Some of our friends think she should try for beauty queen in our state," Mrs. Woods said, "but her father doesn't like the idea."

"No, I don't," Mr. Woods said.

"I agree with you, Mr. Woods," I said. "It would be a pity."

Allegra came in at this moment. She had been sleeping, and her cheeks were rose pink. She had put on a white sleeveless frock, short and tight, and only a young pretty girl could have suffered its severity. She is pretty—I have to grant that. And I can see how my tall dark son might fall in love with her. Ah, but I hope not deeply!

"Speak to the company, sweetie pie," Mrs. Woods said. It was pitiful and touching to see how the parents adored this child, their only one.

"Hello, Mrs. MacLeod," Allegra said with a quick smile.

"I'm afraid Rennie kept you up too late, last night," I said. "I scolded him for it."

"Oh, I can always sleep," Allegra said. She sat on the couch beside her father and he put his arm around her shoulders and squeezed her against him.

"How's my honey?"

"Just fine," Allegra said and leaned her fair head against his shoulder.

"You shouldn't sit up so late. It's like Mrs. MacLeod says."

She pouted at him and did not answer and he squeezed her again. Mrs. Woods watched them tenderly. "They're such chums," she murmured, adoring them both as her possessions.

Nevertheless they were anxious for me to be gone. They would not talk to the child before me. I got up and bade them good-bye, making no haste, as if nothing important had happened, as though we had not rearranged two lives. We lingered on the porch, the three of them following me. We admired the sweet Williams along the path. There is no view from their house, just the path and the flowers and the white gate in the fence. And so I went home. And when Rennie came in to supper I said nothing at all of what I had done. He ate in a hurry and in his work clothes, and then rushed to his room to bathe and change. In a few minutes he raced through the kitchen in clean blue jeans and a fresh shirt.

"Good night, Mom," he called as he went.

"Good night, son," I said.

He went to his rendezvous, and when I had washed the dishes and had settled Baba for the night, I went to my room and locked the door. Tonight I would not sit up. Tonight I could sleep. Whatever I had to meet, I would face it in the morning.

"She has gone," Rennie said.

I waked early and got up immediately, knowing what awaited me. When I came downstairs he sat there at the kitchen table. He had made a pot of coffee and was drinking it, black and strong.

"You haven't been to bed," I said.

He blazed at me. "How could I sleep?"

I sat down and poured myself a cup of coffee. "Go

on. Say whatever you want to say. Let's have it out."

My son was terrible to see. His face was pale and his eyes were burning black. His lips were parched and bitten.

"You went to her parents. You told them."

"Nothing but the truth," I said quietly.

"You wouldn't wait until they knew me!"

Oh, what bitterness in his voice. How hard, how hard to hear it!

"It is better for them to know the truth first," I said. "If she loves you enough to defy her parents, I will say nothing—I swear I will not."

"At least you might have warned me," he cried.

I would not yield to him. "I had to see how they felt, and see it with my own eyes. What they feel cannot be overcome unless your love and hers are equal. I know—I know!"

"She does love me," he muttered. "She told me so."

"She loves you all she can, but it is not enough. It will never be enough, because she is small—small, I tell you! I do not blame her. She cannot help what she is born. But you are born big—as big as the world."

"Damn you," he whispered.

I looked at him. "Now I am glad your father is not here."

We stared at each other.

"Some day you will thank me," I said and wished I had not. It is the common speech of parents. My mother said it to me when she tried to keep me from marrying Gerald. But we had already loved each other, and nothing could keep us apart. I knew, and I defied my mother. "I shall never thank you if you keep us apart," I told her.

And I was right, not she. Even though the letter is

locked in my desk, and though I never see my Gerald's face again I was right and she was wrong.

I kept looking at my son's face and his gaze broke, he so young, so proud in such grief.

"Why did you ever give me birth?" he muttered, and then he sobbed once and leaped from the room.

The house is too still. I knew when I opened my eyes this morning that Rennie was gone. It was a gray morning, a soft rain drifting over the trees and misting into my open window. The curtains hung limp. I listened. It was well past dawn and time for milking. By now I should hear Rennie stirring somewhere. I got up and closed the window and stood looking down the valley half-hidden by rain, summoning my courage to go to his room. I tried to think of Gerald but my heart did not call and his did not answer. I could not see his face and when I forced the eyes of my mind toward him, I saw only the stretching miles of land and the terrible gray sea between us.

To Rennie's room then I went, I opened the door and looked in. The bed was empty, neatly made but empty. All the room was neat and I was frightened by such order. On any other morning his clothes would have been piled up on the armchair, his shoes scattered, his books open on the table. It was only when he left his room that he made it neat, and never neat as it was now. I ran across the room to his closet lest it be empty too. But it was not. Oh, what joy to see his clothes still hanging there! I counted his suits, the brown second best, his work clothes, the jackets and slacks. No, his best dark-blue suit was gone.

Then I saw the book on his desk, closed but with

an envelope in it. It was addressed to me. *Mother.*
Mother? Not Mom—

I sat down to read it because I was too weak to
stand. "Dear Mother," Rennie said to me. "I have
gone to find Allegra. I have to be alone with her and
see for myself why she has changed—if she has. Don't
get in touch with me—don't telephone, don't write. See
you when I can get home again. Rennie."

For Allegra's parents took her away the day after
we talked. Rennie has scarcely spoken to me since.
Now there is nothing to do but wait. Blessings on
old Baba, who is all I have left! I went back to my
room and bathed and dressed and descended to the
kitchen and made myself breakfast. How curious my
life is—how lonely. Loneliness is what I feel here in
my own land. Everyone is lonely, pursuing his lonely
way. We do not confide, we do not share. The very
size of the land divides us. I am as far from Kansas
and that shack where Baba was lost, for he was really
lost, as I am from Peking—nay, farther, for I have my
memories to travel upon across the seas.

And then I was disturbed by plaintive sounds from
upstairs, and I heard Baba's voice. I went upstairs at
once. He lay in his bed, the covers drawn tight about
his neck, his dark eyes bewildered.

"I can't get up," he murmured.

"Are you in pain, Baba?" I asked.

"No pain," he said indistinctly.

"Lie still," I said. "I will send for the doctor."

So I went to the telephone and dialed and it was
early and Bruce Spaulden had not left home.

"Yes?" His voice was crisp.

"Bruce, I think Baba has had another stroke."

"I'll be over."

"Shall I do anything?"

"No, just keep him covered and quiet."

I put up the receiver and went back to Baba and told him that Bruce was coming and then I made the room tidy. Baba is very clean. He is so old that his flesh has no odor. It is ash clean. He lay there, quiet and good, and watched me and I saw his face beginning to draw toward the left. He felt it too and tried to tell me.

"Never mind," I said. "Bruce will be here soon."

I do not open Baba's window at night. There is little warmth in his body and he draws his breath lightly. But the morning had become glorious and I opened the window and the sunshine flowed in for a few minutes and the air was enlivened. Then I closed the window again.

Now I heard Bruce's footsteps in the hall downstairs and he came upstairs and into the room.

"Good morning, Elizabeth," he said.

It was the first time he had called me by my name and I was startled.

"Good morning," I said. "Here is my poor Baba waiting."

Baba turned piteous eyes toward the doctor.

Bruce sat down by the bed and made his examination. There is something wonderful in the way a good doctor examines his patient, his mind concentrated, his hands sure in exploration. I stood respectful, admiring Bruce. He is very American. I wonder why he has never married. He would make a good husband for a woman of integrity and sensitive enough to understand him. He is lean, as most Vermonters are, tall, and serious when he is grave. It is difficult to remember the color of his eyes—gray, I think, changing toward blue. His hair is brown, an ordinary brown, and straight, and his nose is straight and his mouth is firm. When he smiles his face changes altogether. It is quietly mischievous and almost gay. He is even-tempered, inclined to silence and meditation, all good qualities in a husband. I have absorbed a Chinese curiosity into my being and I wanted to ask him why he was not married. To a Chinese mind, anything can be asked, as between friends.

He covered Baba carefully. "Not too serious," he said. "There will be more of these little shocks. Let him rest. He'll sleep a lot. Let him sleep."

Indeed Baba was already sleeping, breathing softly aloud. We left him there and went downstairs into the living room.

"Have you had breakfast?" I asked.

"No," Bruce said.

"Nor have I. So let us breakfast together. I'm lonely because Rennie has gone—"

"Gone?"

"For only a few days, I hope, but I don't know."

And I told him about Allegra. Bruce smiled rather grimly. "He'll be back. We always come back to our mothers. Unless the girl is like you, so you aren't needed!"

"I am sure Allegra is not like me," I said.

I was busy getting the breakfast on the table. Eggs for him, two to my one, and the hens are laying well and I am glad of that. I dislike hens but I like fresh eggs and one cannot be had without the other. Coffee and toast and fruit—I would have my usual good breakfast, let Rennie do what he would.

When we were sitting at the table, I at the end,

since it is my table, and Bruce at the side, I asked my question.

"Because I am so happily married, Bruce, I ask why you have never married."

"Too busy," he said, buttering toast.

"It's not my business—but—"

"Go on," he said. "I lead a simple life. No secrets."

"Wouldn't a wife actually save you time?"

"No. I'd have to think about her—be a companion."

"Are you happy as you are?"

"I don't know. I suppose so. I haven't asked my-self."

I poured his second cup of coffee. What he did not wish to tell he would not tell, however I asked. That is a Vermonter, too.

When he was gone, suddenly and to my own sur-prise I gave myself over to weeping for Gerald and for him only. It has been months since I wept, and even as I was weeping, I knew it was useless. The doors of the house in Peking are shut against me.

I crept upstairs to look at Baba and found him deeply asleep. Even he does not need me now.


. . . This morning, coming home from my Saturday shopping, a small business now that I am alone, for Baba has returned to the food of childhood and sel-dom eats more than milk and bread or rice and a little fruit, I was charmed by the sight of a black mother ewe and her twin white lambs, cropping green grass in a roadside pasture. The sight gave me a small inex-plicable pleasure and I stopped the car and got out merely to watch the mother and her children. The sunlight was bright and mild, Vermont sunshine, never hot as the Chinese sun was hot. The spot was lonely and I sat down on a round gray rock. At this the mother ewe was gently alarmed and bleated softly. Immediately the baby lambs came to her side and stood trembling on their slender legs, and peered at me.

"Don't be afraid of me—"

Now I am really too lonely, for the words come out of my mouth aloud. And I am too lonely, for the next thought was that I would like to own the black ewe and her white lambs and have them live with me. They can crop the short grass on the hillside about my house and keep the semblance of a lawn.

Upon decision I went to find the farmer who owns the ewe and after some search I found not a farmer but one of the wry individuals who cling to the soil of Vermont, a man who farms a little and tinkers somewhat more at whatever job comes his way. He waits in poverty until the job comes and when it is offered he may not even put forth his hand to grasp it. This man was of that breed. He was puttering at mending an unpainted kitchen table when I came from behind his small frame house, neatly painted white with green shutters. He was bending over his work and he straightened when he saw me.

"Well?" he inquired without good morning.

"I'd like to know if your black ewe and white lambs are for sale," I said, also without greeting.

"Might be," he said.

"How much will you take for them?" I asked.

I do not doubt that he knows who I am, the widow woman from over the mountain, or as good as widow, since her husband is in China. But he made no sign of knowledge.

"Don't know as I want to sell," he said, and measured his ruler against a strip of wood.

"I don't know that I want to buy," I said. "Yet maybe I might, to keep the grass down around the house."

"I'll think it over," he said.

"Do," I said. "I'll be at home this afternoon."

He did not come that afternoon, of course, since I had designated it, but he did come this morning, two days later, leading the ewe and the lambs on a dirty rope.

"Ten dollars in cash and the rest in maple syrup," he announced.

We argued for a half hour or so over the quantity of syrup but I yielded, since, being a Vermonter, he would not, and now the ewe and the lambs are cropping the grass on my hillside. The ewe did not settle down at once and I have the rope around her neck and the other end tied to the apple tree, but she is less alarmed than she was, and in a few days I can throw the rope away. And it is quite true that she, with the lambs, do provide me with a comfort I cannot fathom. It is a small comfort, but deep, a mother tie to this earth. I own something more, something alive. I shall have to attach myself by all these small cords lest I be rootless, now that the tap root is gone. No, it is not gone, but it is not here. It is buried far away in my life with Gerald and our love. I have somehow to plant again with this soil. Can this be done when I am alone? I have no word from Rennie.

. . . "I am not religious," I once told Gerald.

This was when he said one doubting evening, "But will you be satisfied with the Chinese gods?"

"Are you?" I asked.

"I have learned to live in two ways," he replied. "There are days when I believe in no gods. There are other days when I believe in all gods."

"Of the two, I shall probably learn to believe in all gods," I said.

A woman in love loses herself and I lost myself. I longed to believe what Gerald believed, to worship as he worshiped. When I found that he worshiped not at all, his belief a matter of mind and will and not the deep involuntary movement of the soul, I did not discuss further the matter of God. Sometimes wandering the Chinese country roads outside our city, we came upon a peasant standing in quiet reverence before a small wayside shrine. Inside the shrine two gods sat, male and female, a married pair, for so the peasants conceive their gods to be. They cannot imagine a solitary god, a male without a female. That, they believe, would be against the law of life. So before the divine pair the peasant stood to light a stick of incense and speak in his heart a wish. It was a sight simple and good.

I said to Gerald, "Would that we could pray in this fashion and believe!"

"It is not that we cannot believe," he replied. "It is that we do not want anything enough. Faith rises from necessity. We have no necessity."

This is true. For out of my necessity now, I find that I must pray. Out of my intense anxiety for my son I have gone each night to his room and standing in the dreadful empty silence I pray for him. How far the prayer rises I cannot guess. Whether there is a listening ear I do not know. But at least the prayer crowding my heart to agony is released and I am relieved. I believe, out of my necessity, that some of the burden is lifted.

Thus far I have resisted the possibility of lifting the receiver of the telephone and calling Allegra's home. It would be easy to ask, "Is Rennie there?" and then, "May I speak to him?" But I will not. It is not only that he would not forgive me. It is also that I must learn to live alone.

At this moment I heard Baba calling. I went to him and found him on the floor. He had slipped to the floor in getting out of bed and he lay there pleasantly helpless, wondering how he got there. He lives from moment to moment, not concerned beyond his present need. He had waked, he had decided to get up and then he fell. I helped him to his feet, and he waved me away. Uncertain as he is in every movement he will not let me stay near him while he washes himself and puts on his garments. Only when he has the Chinese robe about him does he call upon me to fasten the buttons at his collar. So I waited outside his door, and when he called I went in again and buttoned his collar and he declared himself ready for his noonday breakfast. He is happy, he is serene, he has no fears, no anxieties, no need to worship or to pray. A small damage to his brain, the explosion of a minute blood vessel, Bruce tells me, has relieved him of every care. Who says the gods are not kind?

. . . Rennie has come home. When I had ceased to rebel, when my heart grew quiet and when I was resigned and I no longer prayed, then the divine perversity of the universe granted me favor. He came last night, late. I was asleep but I wake at the slightest sound in the house. I heard a door open, the kitchen door. I had locked it as usual, since I am alone, and no one except Rennie has a key. So I knew it was he. The next sound then would be the refrigerator, opened and shut. . . . Yes, that sound, too, I heard. What should I do? I longed to spring from my bed and run downstairs and enfold him. But in my loneliness I had grown cautious. It was no longer what I wished to give but what he would accept. He had gone away once and so, now and forever, it would be easy to go again. He had learned to live without me and without his home. I would not go downstairs. Let him think me asleep. In the morning he could surprise me, and I would pretend surprise. The days of childhood communion were over.

I did not move, I did not stir. I did not set foot upon the floor. In my bed I lay, the faint moonlight streaming across the counterpane, and I listened. He ate at the kitchen table. I heard the clink of a dish and the scrape of a chair. He ate well, for it was a full half hour, perhaps more, before I heard the door to the stair open, the little winding back stair that goes only to his room. I heard the sound of water running into the bath tub cautiously and at half cock, so as not to wake me. Then he did not want me to wake. I had decided wisely. I would not go to his room, not even to gaze at him asleep. But oh, how thankful was I that he had come home! My heart climbed out of my bosom toward heaven in thankfulness. Thank God, thank God!

When all was quiet I would sleep. So I told myself, yet how could I sleep until I knew how he was? Yet I would not go to see. Though he lay there in his bed, only a room beyond mine, he was as far from me at this moment, or nearly, as Gerald was in Peking. A wall was between my son and me. He had become a man, and I knew it. I must wait for him to tell me what he wanted to be to me. Perhaps he does not need a mother, perhaps he wants only a friend, an older woman friend, one who merely happened once to be his mother.

I waited, the hour creeping slowly by and I imagined hours until I looked at the bedside clock. Only an hour and ten minutes had passed. Then I heard the door handle turn softly. I lay motionless and did not light the lamp. When I saw him standing there in the doorway, wrapped in his old red wool bathrobe, I spoke as easily as if he had never been away.

"Is that you, Rennie?"

Though who else could it be? But in such foolish words great moments are encompassed. And he answered as easily.

"How are you, Mother?"

"I am well. Did you just get back?"

"I had something to eat downstairs."

He came toward the bed and sat down on the edge of it, and we gazed at each other in the moonlight.

"Shall I put on the light?" I asked.

"No," he said. "Let's just sit like this. Unless you want to sleep. Did I wake you?"

"Perhaps you did," I said, pretending to be sleepy. "It doesn't matter. I don't get up as early as I used to. Matt milks the cows."

"Is everything all right?" he asked.

I strove for indifference. "I've bought a black ewe and twin white lambs so that I need not cut the grass."

"I saw them in the moonlight."

Then it seemed we had nothing more to say. I would not let a question escape from the prison of my heart. Whatever he wished to tell me I must accept as answer. But nothing prepared me for what he said next.

"You haven't asked me where I have been, Mother."

"You might have written me," I said.

"I couldn't," he said. "And it doesn't matter where I've been. . . . Mother, why did you let me be born? I asked you before."

"You didn't wait for my answer," I reminded him.

"I will wait, now," he said.

He is the one to ask the questions, not I. I can only answer as honestly as possible.

"Your father and I love each other with all our hearts and when there is such love between two young and healthy human beings, one a man, the other a woman, a child is their hope."

"You might have thought what it would mean to me."

Oh what a bitter cry this was!

"It is only fair to your father to tell you that he thought of it and that I denied the need. I said that our child would be so strong, so beautiful, so self-sufficient, that he would meet any situation and be the conqueror."

His eyes were as black as dead coals set in the pale cream face.

"When I was in China," he said, "they called me a foreigner. I did not care then, for I thought I had a country—another country. I thought it was America."

"People have been kind to you here," I said, my tongue and lips as dry as pith.

"It is not kindness I want—it is love."

"You have much love," I said. "Your father loves

you and I love you. And love will come to you from others, some day from a woman."

"Allegra is not allowed to love me," he said. "Her parents forbid it."

"Can she not be disobedient?" I inquired. "My mother forbade me to love your father, too, but I disobeyed. And I have never been sorry."

No, I am not sorry, though Gerald's last letter lies upstairs in my locked box, a thing alive with sorrow. I know he will never write me again.

"Not all women are strong," Rennie said and he looked at me with something like distaste. "And because a woman is not strong," he went on, "it does not mean that her love is the less valuable."

"What is Allegra afraid of?" I tried to hide my scorn.

"She is not afraid of me," he said. "She is afraid of what I carry in my veins, the genes, the ancestry, the irremovable part of me, that which I cannot change."

"You mean the Chinese part of you," I said.

He nodded, and he knotted his hands together. His hands are all American, not smooth and pale as Gerald's are, but hard and strong at the knuckles.

"I thought so," I said. "The very part of you that I love most and am most proud of because I love your father, you wish you did not have. Shame on you, Rennie!"

"You don't understand," he cried. "You are American, your ancestry is pure—"

"Oh, pure," I cried back at him. "The rebels of half a dozen nations in Europe, the renegade young son of an English lord and an Irish girl, a crafty Dutch merchant who cheated the Indians out of their land, a strain of German—"

"None of that matters," he said stubbornly. "You are all white."

I yielded. It was not the moment for argument.

"Say what you please," I said.

"I am going to Kansas," he went on. "I'll work on Sam's ranch this summer, and go to college in the autumn. Sam will get me a scholarship."

No "if you please," no "if you don't mind, Mother," no "unless you need my help here at home." But I am proud too and I do not ask my son's help.

"I wonder that you came home to tell me," I said.

"So that you know," he said, his jaw as hard as iron.

There was my fate laid out before me, and I must take it with both hands and without complaint.

"When will you go?" I asked.

"I suppose I ought to stop long enough to see Baba," he replied.

"A little longer," I protested.

Perhaps it is time for me to tell him of Baba's wife, his grandmother. Some of this rebel blood in him comes from her. She suffered, too, because she was not loved. Perhaps she can help him now as I cannot.

"Stay a day, at least, Rennie. There are things I want to say to you before you go—things I have never told you."

He looked at me quickly with those dark, dark eyes.

"All right," he said, "if that's the way you want it—"

. . . Where will I find a home for my son? Where can he find the country to be his own?

When Baba woke the next morning we went upstairs. There he was, lying upon his pillows exactly as he had gone to sleep, his white hair scarcely ruffled, his dark eyes vague and only half open. I spoke to him.

"Baba, good morning. See who has come to you."

He opened his eyes and stared at us. "Who is that?"

"You know."

"Is it Gerald?"

"No—no—no. It is Rennie."

He did not know Rennie. He has forgotten his own grandson. He moved his lips. "Should I know him?" he inquired at last.

"Yes, you should," I said. "He is Gerald's son—and mine."

"Gerald's son," he mused. "Had Gerald a son?"

I turned to implore. "Rennie, forgive him. He is so old. He has forgotten everything."

Oh, what a look of sadness was on the young face!

"It doesn't matter," Rennie said. "Nothing matters."

"Go to sleep again, Baba," I said. "I will come back soon." We tiptoed out again, and I knew that I had lost. Baba, in innocence, has deserted me and mine. He has withdrawn from us into the distances of old age.

Then I was frantic to reclaim my son. "Rennie, come into my room now. I have pictures to show you. I must show them to you before you go."

He followed me quietly, and in my room he sat down as formally as a guest and waited. And I took out my box of pictures and found the one of Gerald's mother.

"This is the Chinese lady Baba married," I told him. "This is your grandmother, your father's mother. She is quite beautiful, in her own dignified way. She is someone to be proud of, the daughter of an ancient family rooted in Peking. You remember your great-uncle, Han Yu-ren, surely."

Rennie took the picture and gazed at the calm Chinese face. "Why did Baba marry her?"

"He wanted to—to become part of the country to which he had dedicated his life. He thought he could get near to the people he loved. He wanted to—to cease to be foreign."

"Now he has forgotten everything," Rennie said. "He does not know even me. I suppose he never loved her."

"Why do you say so? You don't know."

"If he loved her he would have remembered me."

I could not deny it. However old I grow, whatever the change in body and mind, while I draw breath I shall not forget Gerald, nor Gerald's son.

"Baba did what he thought was right," I said.

"It is not enough," Rennie said. "There has to be love."

And he gave me back the picture. Now he got to his feet and leaned down from his height and kissed my cheek.

"Good-bye, Mother," he said. He went away immediately. I heard his old car whirl down the road in a cloud of summer dust. This time he may never come back. I do not know. What I remember is that he spoke again as his father taught him, his English classic and pure. The slang, the American boy talk, he had wiped from tongue and lips. What this means also I do not know.

I cannot go away, I cannot follow Rennie even if I would, for here is Baba, who has no one but me. I am held on this quiet farm, remote from everyone except Matt and his wife, and they have lived so long together in the valley that they know only the language of a hate-filled love. They quarrel and enjoy themselves in combat by day and I do not doubt also by night. Indeed I am sure that their chief conflict is by night in the great old double bed that fills the small bedroom on the north side of the kitchen. Seven children they have bred together, and each of them the fruit of a quarrel. They have needed no other companionship, no other excitement, I do believe. Matt is insanely jealous and Mrs. Matt is proud of his jealousy, boasting of its oppression.

"If Matt so much as sees a man's hat in the house, he takes conniptions," so she boasts. "Oh, I pay for it, I do," she declares, and her little round wrinkled face glows with pleasure.

She said that this morning when in a stupor of loneliness I crossed the dusty road to praise her flower beds. Before I could reply as I always do, that she is lucky Matt still cares enough about her to be jealous, the postman passed and I cried good-bye and ran after him. There in the shade of the big maple at the gate he paused and handed me a few letters, none of any importance except a thin gray envelope. It was sent from Singapore. I knew the stamp, but the handwriting was strange.

"Your husband?" the postman asked.

"No," I said, and then was afraid of what might be written within and so I left him and went to the rock beside the spring, and sat there in the shade of a leaning apple tree and tore open the envelope.

"Dear Elder Sister," the letter began.

It was from her.

All these months I have not answered Gerald's letter. He asked my permission and I have not given it.

Underneath all that I do has been the knowledge of this delay, a secret as hidden as a sin. Now I cannot hide it any longer.

She writes in English, but not well. She is trying to convey something to me. She wants me to understand that she will not enter my house to take my place until I give permission.

You have lived in Peking very long [she writes]. I think you understand something very much about us Chinese people. Here now it is hard for living, nevertheless. It is also hard for MacLeod, your husband, and he is wishing so much for some woman to take care of house and mending and cooking, and so forth. At my former request, he wrote to you asking your agreement to my coming to his house as wife-in-absence. You know this is quite common, no more second wife or concubine, as before, which is too old-fashioned, but wife-in-absence. Of course if you come back some other time, I will go away if you wish. To you I have respect as younger to elder. Please permit me, and tell me how everything should be in caring for our husband. I wish to do what you tell me and make him so happy. This is my duty. But first your permission, please, to save his life. I send this letter to a secret friend in Singapore and please return to same.

Your humble younger sister,

MEI-LAN

The address in Singapore is to a silk shop. Someone there, I suppose, is her secret friend, someone in touch with this strange new China, by which I am rejected. I wish I had the courage to write boldly to

Gerald. But what would I write? Shall I give my permission for another woman to take my place? And can she take my place? Surely no American woman has ever been in like predicament.

This rock farm of mine, in this distant state of Vermont, is as far from Gerald now as though he did not exist. Perhaps it is I who no longer exist. Why indeed should I exist who am no longer needed—or loved? Or am I loved? I cannot answer this letter today. I am voiceless, I cannot think. I do not know what to say, until I am in communion with him again.

I come to my room. I take his letter from my locked box and though I have sworn that I will not look at it again, I do so. I set it down here. I copy every word, and so make his words my own. I shall never forget them now. This is the letter from Peking, Gerald's last letter.

My DEAR WIFE:

First before I say what must be said, let me tell you that I love only you. Whatever I do now, remember that it is you I love. If you never receive a letter from me again, know that in my heart I write you every day. I say this because of what I must next tell you. It is imperative for me to take into my home a Chinese woman. It is not only that I need someone to look after the house, to wash my clothes, mend and so on. You know very well how helpless I am in all these matters where you have been so useful to me. But it is necessary now for me to prove myself. It is not enough, it seems, for me to swear loyalty to those in present power. I must forswear all my past, I must curse my non-Chinese blood and declare against the foreign part of myself.

I have been ordered to choose another woman. I tell you because you and I have always been honest, one with the other. If I were to be less than honest with you now, it would mean that I had indeed forgotten our life together. I shall never forget and so I tell you.

I cannot write again. It would be too dangerous for me and too dangerous even for our son. You think him safe in your country, but he is not safe anywhere unless I repudiate him and you. If you hear I have done so publicly, do not believe I have done so in reality. I wish to stay alive, if possible, until these days are past. If I meet death in spite of all my efforts to avoid it, remember that my only thought is of you, my Eve.

GERALD

I must of course give permission. I do not know why I have delayed all these months to do what I knew had to be done. Now that this letter has come from the woman, and I know that she has not gone to him, I see that I must give permission at once. Perhaps I shall cable. No, that would be too startling. To receive a cable from America might make trouble for a Chinese even in a British colony. I will write and send the letter air mail. So I write. I copy my letter here that I may always know what I said. If ever Gerald and I meet again, here is the record. For I am really writing for Gerald. Yes, dear and beloved, I am writing this for you. If you cannot come to me nor I to you, then it may be possible nevertheless some day to send you the record. I wish I had said to you on that last day that you too must keep the record. Ah no, it would not be safe there, where you are. The servants may be paid by others than you. Here in this quiet Vermont valley there are no spies. I think there are no spies. I write my letter to Mei-lan. And now it occurs to me that she did not sign her family name. Mei-lan is a common name, impossible to trace. But her name does not matter.

DEAR YOUNGER SISTER:

Your letter has come to my hand. I have read it. I give my permission. You may not take my place, for each woman has her own place in a man's life, but you may enter my house and make your own place there. I shall tell no one here in my country, for none would understand. It is true, as you say, that I understand. Nevertheless, my heart breaks. Care for him well, for I love him.

ELIZABETH

I stamped the envelope myself and took it to the post office and slipped it into the box under the window. But Miss Myra saw it. She is our postmistress, a plump friendly woman, and, being unmarried, consumed with curiosity about marriage, and especially about mine.

"Letter to your husband?" she inquired gaily. She has pink round cheeks withered in many fine lines, and a tight little pink mouth and two round blue eyes without eyebrows. Her hair is frizzed and yellow.

"No, not to my husband," I said.

She took the letter from the box and studied it. "A foreign address. China, ain't it?"

"No, Singapore, a British colony."

"I thought they hadn't any colony now."

118

"They returned India to the Indians, but they still hold Hongkong and Singapore."

"Do they now!"

She looked unbelieving but I said no more. I had done what I must and I went home. Baba was not yet out of bed, his day beginning at noon and ending at twilight. He seemed drowsy, vague, uncomprehending, and I did not, as sometimes I do, endeavor to rouse him. But when he was dressed and sitting in his armchair, for he no longer comes downstairs, when he had eaten his bowl of oatmeal and drunk a cup of tea, he suddenly seemed awake and knowing. Perhaps Rennie had left a dart of memory in him, by which he was pricked.

"Did someone come here yesterday?" he inquired.

"Yes, Baba. It was Rennie."

He mused. "Rennie—who is Rennie?"

"Your grandson, Baba."

He reflected upon this information without speaking. A half hour later, while I was straightening his room, he spoke with sudden clarity.

"But I thought it was Ai-lan."

"How could it be, when she was a woman and Rennie is a man—very nearly?"

I spoke half-playfully, while I dusted his table.

"She looked like a man," he said. "She put on a uniform. It was of dark-blue cotton, the jacket buttoned, and trousers like a man. It startled me."

"It must have been startling—on a woman."

I listened now. So Rennie looks like his Chinese grandmother! He looks like Gerald, certainly. Then Gerald looks like his mother. In Peking they said he looked like his father. But that is the way it is. Each

119

side insists the other side prevails and so each rejects what is not like itself.

"Ai-lan was killed," Baba said painfully. His old face wrinkled and tears dripped down from his eyes.

"It was long ago, Baba."

"I believe it was not," he replied. "I believe it was only last year, or at most two years ago. Her grave is still fresh." He paused. "Where is her grave?" he asked.

He was determined to weep for his dead wife. But why now, after all the years?

"Did you love her, Baba?" I asked.

He paused to consider. When he spoke it was in one of his rare moments of clarity.

"I couldn't love her," he said. "I tried, for the Scriptures say a man must cleave to his wife. They do not say how it is to be done. And she knows I could not."

"You gave her a son," I reminded him for comfort.

"Ah, but she knew," he retorted. "She knew very well. On the morning he was born, and at an unusual hour, I believe, at ten o'clock on a fine spring morning, I went into her room when the doctor told me I should do so. She lay with the child sleeping on her arm. 'I have given you a son.' That was what she said. And I couldn't speak. The child had long black hair. It was a shock to think my son was Chinese. I wasn't prepared."

I tried to laugh. "Baba, the mother was Chinese—your wife!"

But he shook his head in vague, remembered distress.

"I was not prepared," he insisted.

What he meant was that he had not thought of a child. He married Gerald's mother for reasons of his own and not for a son. He did not want him. And that not being wanted had remained deep in Gerald's being, a dagger never withdrawn, a wound never healed. It was the dagger and the wound that kept Gerald from coming with me to my country. I see it, I feel it. But Rennie carries the mark and he is here. Oh, how deep is the wound of not being loved! From generation to generation the newborn heart is wounded afresh and cannot be healed until love is found, in someone, somewhere.

Baba had begun to weep again, and I asked, to divert him, "Baba, do you remember Sam Blaine?"

He was diverted. He was doubtful. "Do I know him?"

"You lived in his little house, in Kansas."

"Did I?"

"Yes, and I tell you because Rennie has gone there to live and work on the ranch. Sam Blaine was in China during the war. He liked it and he liked the people. They were kind to him. That is why he was kind to you when you were taken ill on the train and they put you off. Sam Blaine happened by somehow —I must ask how, someday—and became your friend. Now he is Rennie's friend."

He remembered none of it, but at least he forgot to weep. I pushed his chair to the window where he likes to sit, and he gazed peacefully out upon the rising hills and the valleys. He likes the sheep, and he leaned forward now and again, to see where they were cropping the grass.

"I shall be back soon," I said, and went away to do my day's work.

. . . Tonight when Baba was in bed and ready for sleep he suddenly remembered very much about Sam

Blaine. I had all but closed the door, I had said good night, when Baba spoke.

"About Sam Blaine—"

"Yes?"

"Sam Blaine is forty-two years old. He has never married. His father owned two thousand acres of good black earth. He was a cattle man, and he owned two mines in Nevada, too. His wife died when the child was only two years old. Sam was his only child."

"Baba," I cried, "how well you remember!" So I came back into the room and sat down and Baba said he had been taken from the train, ill and feverish, and told to wait in the railroad station, and Sam Blaine had come to fetch some freight. Instead he took Baba home with him and put him to bed.

"I had typhoid fever," Baba said. "I was very ill. Sam stayed with me in the hut."

And bit by bit he told me the story. When he woke in the night, not knowing where he was, Sam sat by the bed and talked about China. He spoke of Chinese villages and country roads and how the nightingales sing in the twilight of summer days. He was there during the war, but he did not speak of war or death. Instead he spoke to Baba of peaceful scenes, of families sitting in the doorways of their homes at evening, of men tilling the fields, of women at the pond washing the clothes.

When he repeated these things to me, Baba was suddenly bewildered. He looked at me with troubled eyes, his face that of a tired old child.

"Where is that land where we once lived?" he asked.

"It is where it always was," I said. "It is across the sea. And Gerald is there."

He was puzzled. "Then why are we here?"

Why, indeed? My heart broke and I leaned my head on his bony old breast.

"Now it is you who are weeping," he said and he lay patient and still, waiting for me to lift up my head from his breast. There was no warmth in him, only a final patience, and my tears dried and I lifted my head.

"It is time for you to sleep," I told him.

"And will you sleep?" he asked.

"Sooner or later I, too, will sleep," I promised and I drew the blanket about his shoulders and went away.


. . . Oh, the awful silence of the valley at night! No one comes near me and I am as alone as though I lived solitary upon a planet. Here and there in the distance a light burns. It means a house, a home, two people, perhaps children. The oil lamp burns yellow in Matt's little house, and far down at the end of the valley the bright single light is the naked electric bulb that never goes out above the office door of Bruce Spaulden. I know, too, the intermittent flares of summer folk. None of them burns for me. Sometimes I light every lamp in my empty house and a stranger passing by could believe the house is full of guests. But I have no guests.

Tonight, when loneliness became intolerable, I went upstairs, and took down the box of Gerald's letters and I laid them out upon my desk in order of time. There are not many—only twelve in all, not including the final one. The first one was written soon after we left him in Shanghai. I wonder now if it was right to leave him. Yet he bade me go. I think he was not yet afraid. Indeed, he was even cheerful, believing that nothing could be worse than the years of war through which we had already passed. He was hopeful about the new government. Those builders of the new order spoke well. We had no presentiments, in spite of old Mr. Pilowski, the White Russian who managed the hotel where we stayed.

"Not to be trusted," Mr. Pilowski declared, and brushed up his stiff mustaches. Black they were, but dyed, of course. Mr. Pilowski must have been well over seventy. "Never are revolutionaries to be trusted —no, not in the world. So they came into my Russia, promising all and seizing everything. So did they in France before, killing the kings and the queens and themselves behaving worsely."

Gerald argued with him. "We can scarcely go on as we are, Mr. Pilowski. The people are wretched after the war. Inflation is crushing. Nothing is being done."

"Some day, you will know that nothing being done is better than wickedness being done," Mr. Pilowski declared. He grew red and angry and Gerald smiled, refusing further argument, but still believing himself right. It is the arrogance of the Chinese, and I must never forget that Gerald is half-Chinese, to believe they are different from all other peoples, more reasonable, more sane, than other peoples are. In some ways it is true.

Gerald's first letter is almost gay. "Everything goes well," he writes. "I am beginning to think you should have stayed in China. Rennie could have taken his college work here in Peking. I do not know why we were so easily frightened. I believe that a new day is coming in this old, old country of mine."

Not "our" old, old country, but "mine." I see now the first hint of separation from me. He was already choosing his country, alone, if need be.

The hopefulness continues through to the fifth letter. Then I see the first hint of doubt.

"My Eve," he writes me, "perhaps it is better that you are away for a year or so. In order to succeed the new government must clear away all obstacles. Do you remember Liu Chin, the silk merchant? It seems he is a traitor. He is so mild, so gentle—do you remember? Today he was shot at the Marco Polo Bridge with eleven others, two of them women. It is inevitable that some do not like the new order. But the new order is here. We must live with it and through it. The Minister of Education unfortunately is not a man of wide education. I am having to replace—" He scratches that out. It appears that already it is not safe to be frank. Thereafter Gerald writes no more of anything of importance. He tells me when the yellow Shantung rose in the east court blooms.

"Dear Eve, the rose is late this year. We have had bitter dust storms, the most severe I have ever known. The goldfish are dying in the pool although I have tried to keep the water fresh. The gardener went home to his parents in Shansi a month ago. I have had difficulty in finding another. People do not want to work—" The words are scratched out again. It is not to be believed. People do not want to work? Why not? Gerald does not say he has had my letters. I wrote every day and mailed the letters once a week.

The eighth letter is very short. "Dear Wife: Today is like any day now in my life. I have made the schedule, and am engaging the professors for next semester. The new dean is a clever young man with many ideas. The dean of women is a former student of mine. She was ambitious even in youth. Tell Rennie to study engineering. It will be better for him than teaching.

Tonight is hot and still. I face a long lonely summer."

The ninth letter is listless. Commencement is over and he is tired. I know the mood. We used to take a journey, make a holiday, go perhaps to the sea at Peitaiho, or travel to the Diamond Mountains in Korea. One year we went to Tai Shan and lived in a Buddhist temple for a month. I wonder if Rennie remembers. The old abbot befriended him, and taught him how to play cat's cradle with a strip of silk.

Three months passed before the tenth letter reached me, and it is an empty letter. I wept when I read it and it makes me weep now. For I see that my beloved has resigned himself to that which he does not understand. "I wonder if I chose wisely in not going with you and our son to America. It is too late now. In case I never see you—" Here he scratches words again.

The eleventh letter is all but final. "Dearly Loved, it is better for us not to plan the day of meeting. It is better to live life as we find it, you on your side of the world, I on mine. Let Rennie become an American citizen. Help him to find a country of his own. If he forgets me let it be so."

It is easy to see the story now. He is a prisoner. The city he chose has become his cell. He is no longer free. And I am not free because I love him. As long as he lives I shall not be free. . . . Let me be glad that at least a woman is at his side. Though she be not I, he has someone with him. So why do I weep?

And I continue to weep.

. . . This morning Baba frightened me by a fainting fit. He got up as usual and ate his slight breakfast, now only orange juice, a spoonful of porridge and hot milk. Then, in the midst of thanking me as he is careful to do, he crumpled in his chair. I sent Matt in a hurry for Bruce Spaulden, and lucky it was that Matt was near by, trimming the hemlock hedge. Meanwhile I stood beside Baba's chair, not daring to move him, and frightened lest Bruce be already started on his rounds and therefore inaccessible.

Lucky again he was not. He came running up the gravel walk from the gate, hatless and without his coat, his bag swinging from his hand. The door was open and he entered, and leaped upstairs and into the room, his thin Vermont face without a smile, and his eyes seeing nothing but his patient. I knew better than to speak if I were not spoken to, and I stood silent, waiting his command.

"Pull up his sleeve."

I pulled up Baba's sleeve. Into the slack old flesh of his upper arm Bruce drove the needle quickly and with skill. Then he lifted Baba in his arms and laid him on his bed.

"Cover him and keep him warm," he told me. "There is nothing I can do. He will pull out of it, likely, but one of these days he won't. You aren't to be scared. Even if I were sitting right beside him when it happens I couldn't do anything. I'd give him a shot, of course, as I did today, but it'd be no more than a gesture."

"I'll stay by him until he wakes," I said.

"Not necessary," Bruce said. "Go about your business. Come in every now and then and see how he is."

He was packing his bag while I covered Baba and tucked the quilt about him. The morning was warm for our mountains, but Baba's flesh was cool as the flesh of one newly dead. Yet he breathed.

I looked up to see Bruce watching me.

"Come downstairs," he said.

I followed him down. I thought he was going to the door, but no, he sat down in the hall on the ladder-back chair near the big clock.

"This is no time to ask," he said in his abrupt way. "But I don't know as one time is better than another when a man has something on his mind. . . . Elizabeth, will you marry me?"

He was not joking. For a second I thought he was, but his intense eyes told me better.

"I am married already," I said. "My husband is not dead."

"I didn't know," he muttered. "He never shows up."

"He can't," I said. "He's in Peking, China."

"Might as well be dead," he muttered.

I said, "For me he lives."

Bruce got up and snatched his bag from the floor where he had set it down, and made for the door. There he paused, he turned to look at me. I was at the foot of the stair, holding to the newel post.

"All the same, Elizabeth," he said, his eyes gray under his black brows, "things being what they are in this uncertain world, and in a most uncertain age, my offer holds."

"I wish you hadn't made it," I said. "Now I'll think of it every time I see you."

"Which is exactly as I wish it," he said.

He grinned suddenly, and I looked into a different face, a face almost gay in a sober sort of way. Then he was gone. And I stood there with an odd sort of feeling—not love, not that at all, only a strange pleasant sort of female warmth. For the second time in my life a man had proposed to me. To be honest, I suppose I ought to say that it is the first time, for when Gerald asked me to marry him he was so hesitant, so

doubtful, so fearful lest he was not being fair to me—
he an anonymous sort of human being, as he said,
whose origins were double and from both sides of the
world and so belonging nowhere in particular—that it
was I who coaxed it out of him. I have nothing whatever to do with this proposal that has just been given
to me now. I have never suspected the possibility that
Bruce could love any woman, much less me. He loves
children, that I know, and only with children have I
seen that changeless exterior of his break into something like tenderness. He is almost totally silent. I
can live alone, I am learning to live alone. But I am
not sure that I could live with a silent man.

Stupefied, I left the door open and went back to
Baba. He was still unconscious.

. . . Today the postman brought me a letter bearing
the stamp of the People's Republic of China.

"It must be from your husband," he said, and
handed me the letter as proudly as though he had
fetched it himself from across the westward sea.

"Thank you," I said, and did not tell him that I
knew the moment that I looked at the handwriting
that it was not from Gerald. It was from—what shall
I call her? For I am Gerald's wife. And I cannot use
the word concubine. Yet I suppose that is what she
is. I suppose the Chinese on our street in Peking call
her his Chinese wife and me his American wife. But
the dagger piercing me is this question—if she can
write, why cannot he? Is there some loyalty, or fear,
that prevents him? Is the loyalty to me, that, knowing
how we have loved, he cannot bring himself to ac-
knowledge that he desecrates our love?

I opened the letter and there was the simple handwriting.

DEAR ELDER SISTER:

Your letter has come. I thank you for such answer. Now it is my duty to tell you of our husband. I am not sure that this letter will ever come before your eyes, but I do my duty. I send it in the secret way. If it is found by the wrong person, then you will never see it. But I try. Now I tell you our husband is well but he is sad. He does not talk to me. He goes every day to his office, and at night he comes home. The house is as you left it. I do not change anything. Only I cannot keep it so clean. Sometimes he complains because it is not so clean. I tell him I cannot do all as well as you do. But I cook what he likes to eat. He does not mention your name but he keeps you in his mind as secret joy. In the night when the moon shines he walks into the courts and stares at the moon. Is it the same moon in your country? I have heard it is the same moon. To the moon then he gives his thinking of you.

As to his health, it is good except that he does not sleep much. We have no children. He told me he does not want a child. I said what of me? He said, it is better for you not to have my child because the blood is mixed. But I hope for a child. I go to temple and pray before the Goddess of Childbirth. I go in secret because they tell us not to believe in gods now. Please take care of yourself. If you were here the house would not be lonely as now. We could be friends.

YOUR YOUNGER SISTER

She does not sign her name this time, for safety. And the envelope was not mailed in Singapore but in Hongkong. I feel strangely better for the letter. It is sweet and simple and I am surprised that I am not jealous. When the moon rises over these mountains in Vermont, I shall go out and stand in its light, knowing that a few hours before he has so stood. Thank you, my younger sister.

I live this strange inner life. No one in the valley could possibly understand it even if I could speak of it. And I cannot speak. But now I do most earnestly wish to leave that world in which I lived with Gerald and enter this world to which I am compelled by circumstances as far beyond my power to control as the setting of the sun and the rising of the new moon, at this moment poised above the cedars of the mountain. Yet I cannot leave that world, which actually does not exist for me any more as a practical reality, and so I cannot enter the world in which I am forced to live. Here I exist, in space.

. . . If only I could stop remembering! I long not to remember, for I can feel Gerald cutting one cord after another between us. It is not only that he no longer writes me. He is also denying himself the thought of me. In other times, when there was certainty, or even hope of our meeting again, I could feel his communion with me. On those rough hills of Szechuan, when I was at Chungking and he struggling somewhere across country, on foot, leading his students and professors westward, I could feel, especially at evening, at sunset and at moonrise, the outreaching of his heart and conscious mind, and we were united. But now, though I send myself across land and sea in search of him, I do not find him. He hides himself.

131

He has withdrawn from me. This means but one thing
—he has no hope of ever seeing me again. I do not
believe he has ceased to love me. That is not possible.
It is simply that for us the earthly life is ended. And
yet, I continue in space. I am not freed of the past,
and present and future do not exist.

When Bruce asked me to marry him, the words
reached my ears but not my heart. They echoed in
me. I hear them reverberating and empty. It is only
when I enter Baba's room that meaning comes back
to me, not strong and alive as it was in the house in
Peking, but quiescent and yet there. I feel as one feels
in the presence of ruined palaces and silent gardens,
existing but no longer used and alive. I realize that I
return to Baba's room often for no other purpose than
to see his ancient figure, wrapped in the Chinese robe
of blue brocade silk, sitting by the window. The few
things brought with me from China, a pair of scrolls,
a small jade vase, some porcelain bowls from Kiangsi,
a rug as blue as the northern Chinese sky, have somehow sorted themselves out of the house and into
Baba's room. When I step through that door I close
it behind me.

"Are you all right, Baba?" I ask.

"Quite all right," he says peaceably.

He does not know where he is in the flesh. It is of
no significance. He is somewhere in the world he
knew once and which no longer exists, except for him.
Now and then he asks vaguely of the servants.

"How is it you do not tell the amah to wash my
clothes?"

"Amah is not here, Baba."

"Indeed!"

He does not ask where she is. That would be to risk

a knowledge he cannot face. He falls silent and forgets. There he sits, Gerald's father, a beautiful old man, straight and tall, thin as a saint ascetic, his hair whiter than snow upon the mountain, his white beard uncut. He has forgotten even Rennie. He does not think. He simply is. And it is this elemental existence, pure and childlike and unaware of anything except itself, that compels me to remember Peking.

Oh, that dreamlike city! When I think of Gerald it is to see him in the city of emperors. Everything in life was there, the palaces under their roofs of blue and gold, containing a history, crowded with imperial men and women. In the wide streets the common folk forgot their commonness and took on princely airs because the city in which they live with their ancestors is a kingly city. Even the beggars were not craven. They came out from their corners, hands outstretched but heads held high. I do not remember the city whole. It is too rich with life for that. I see it in the glorious fragments of sunlight piercing the yellow dust of a spring storm. I see it a vast summer garden, blue porcelain roofs and golden ornaments gleaming between the dark of green cedar trees. I see it under snow heavy on the roofs and in the streets, the men and children picking their way as carefully as cats, but cheerfully, their cheeks red with cold and fur caps pulled over their ears. I see the streets at night, gay with festivals, or quiet with the good plainness of daily life, lamps burning, candles lit, families gathered about the supper table, men gossiping over waterpipes, a woman nursing her little child. . . . How still the Vermont mountains are, how empty of human life! The forest, as night falls, grows sinister in darkness. Sometimes the sun shines through the trees upon the brakes and ferns and that underworld appears all innocence and tender beauty. But the sun sets early in the valley and the shadows descend.

It is autumn again, and the leaves are turning. What life is there in the scanty soil on these mountains that sends the sap running in the maple trees in spring and whose withdrawing in the autumn creates colors so bright and naked? The trees bleed with color now as they bleed in March with sap. Yesterday, staying to talk with our state forester, a spare young man intense with mission to the trees, he told me that no one knows why the maple sap runs upward in the spring. This force is not explained, but it is powerful enough to move engines if it were harnessed. It is a cellular force, not directly propelled from the earth through the roots, for if a maple is cut, the sap still runs upward through the trunk. There is no heart in the trees as in the human body, no pump visible and beating, but a pure force, elemental and almost spiritual in its source. It is life force expressed through matter.

The leaves drift down and the mountains emerge in great sweeping outlines against a sky of royal blue. The work on the farm is done for the year, except for the routines of the cows and their calving, the milking twice a day, the feeding and watering of the hens and gathering of eggs from the hen house. I find comfort in the daily tasks, although Matt does not really need me. I sold three cows last month to save winter feed. Matt put up the storm windows and doors yesterday and today the weather immediately turned warm with the same perversity that it used to do in China. But I cannot go out as the Chinese farmers did and shake my fist at the Old Man in the Sky. There was a friendly critical relationship between the Chinese gods and the farming folk. The people expected their gods to look after them and to send rain and sunshine in season. Warm weather after the first festival of winter made the winter wheat grow high and so risk being frozen when the bitter days came. A farmer spoke his mind thus to his gods:

"You old Head up yonder! What reason have you for sending down heat instead of cold? Are you drunk up there in Heaven? Is your brain muddled? Consider yourself! I warn you—no more incense, no more gifts to the temple!"

I am skeptic enough about gods but how can I explain that within two days a blizzard came down from the north? How we laughed, Gerald and I! Oh, we had so much good laughter in our marriage. I had to teach him to laugh, I remember. I had to release his rich Chinese humor. When he was most Chinese he was most gay. I wonder if his Chinese wife can make him laugh. It is her letter I take out now and read, not his. I find I cannot read Gerald's letters to me. They seem old, they belong to another age. Whatever he is now, it is not what I knew. I try to see him through these letters of his Chinese wife, but I see only his shadow.

. . . . Tonight, as I open my window to my narrow valley, a flurry of snow rushes in. I feel the flakes cold upon my face and the wind blows through my nightgown. Hurry into bed, let me draw the warm blankets about my shoulders. I will not remember how lonely I must lie. I will think of the comfort of my blankets. They are made of the wool sheared in July from my sheep. My sheep keep me warm and my cows give

me milk and butter and cheese. My land gives me
food and beauty to look upon. As for the blankets,
when I sent in the bags of wool to the factory, I asked
that they be made double, and dyed a deep pink, and
they came back to me the color of crushed roses. I lie
beneath them with pleasure and I comfort myself
with their warmth and color. My comfort and my
pleasure are in such small things. It is the small things
that are eternal.

. . . Today, while the ground lies white under the
snow and the mountains look twice their height, Rennie's first letter has come to me. It was the only letter
the postman put in the mailbox, and so I had nothing
to divert me from it. I sat down where I was in the
kitchen, I let my broom fall, I threw aside the dusting
cloth and tore open the envelope.

"Dear Mother—"

I kissed the words and went on. He writes as if he
had left home only yesterday instead of being months
away.

But where are you, Rennie? The letter is sent from
a midwestern college. He does not want to go to Harvard, where his father went, he says. He wants to be
only himself, he says. So that is what he is, working
his way as Sam said he would. It is a practical sort of
letter, giving facts and no details. He is studying hard,
he likes physics very much. He is rooming with a boy
named George Bowen. Ah, George Bowen has a sister.
Not pretty? But very intelligent and rather good-look-
ing. Tall, it seems.

"Now, Mother, you are not to get ideas. I am
through with women."

Here I pause. At nineteen my son is through with

women! Oh Allegra, you have hurt him very much. But every man and every woman is hurt by first love, except the rare ones, like Gerald and me, whose first love deepens into the only love.

"I shall be home for Christmas," Rennie writes. Now that is blessed news. That is enough to satisfy me. The boy is coming home and so we shall have a Christmas. It would be too melancholy for Baba and me to think of Christmas. He doubtless has forgotten the day and I could not remember it alone. I know that if Rennie had not sent me this letter I would have let the day slip past, pretending that it was a day like any other. Now I shall make a plum pudding and dress a turkey and insist upon fresh oysters from the grocery store. I shall make walnut candies for Rennie and begin at once to knit him a red sweater. And his clothes not mended all these months! He must bring everything home and let me see what has happened. The house is suddenly full of light and life. I dash upstairs to Baba who is sitting placidly by the window, where I left him.

"My knees are cold," he says to me in Chinese.

"You have let the rug slip to the floor, careless Baba!"

I pretend to scold him, also in Chinese. When he speaks in Chinese he forgets his English. I tell him the heavenly news but in English.

"Rennie is coming home for Christmas, Baba. Can you hear me? Do you understand? Say it after me, 'Rennie is my grandson.'"

He lifts patient old eyes to my face. He repeats in a quavering half-frightened voice, "Rennie is my grandson."

"He is coming home for Christmas."

"Coming home for Christmas," Baba repeats.

I doubt he knows what it means, but he will know when Rennie himself comes in. Oh, he will know, then!

I kiss the top of Baba's head and fly off to inspect Rennie's room. I wonder if Matt can help me paint the walls? A pale yellow, I think—

. . . The days have flown by. It is four days before Christmas and Rennie comes home tonight. Meanwhile I have had two letters written in the Peking house but mailed elsewhere, one in Manila, one in Bangkok. This little Chinese woman is resourceful. I begin to be interested in her. It seems she has friends who mail her letters in widely separate places. She does this, I am sure, so that Gerald may be safe. His letters are watched and read, doubtless, but hers she can slip into her sleeve and take with her to some family where she visits and she is not suspected. I wonder what she looks like. I have wanted, and not wanted, to ask her for a small photograph. But she would send it if she could. She is that sort of a woman, a chatterbox of a woman, cheerful and loving, one who sets store by photographs and keepsakes and such things. She writes of Gerald and the house and what they do. She does not mention his name but we both know who this "He" is.

"He has a cold today. It is the sand that settles in his throat while he talks in the classroom. I have made hot ginger tea and mixed it with honey. He sips it and is better."

Yes, the sands of autumn storms used to make Gerald cough, and then he could not sleep well. We used to think of going to some other part of China far from the distant desert of the northwest, perhaps to one of the great cities on the Yangtse River, but Gerald, when it came to the point of decision, could never leave Peking.

"One belongs to this city as to a country," he said. "There is no other like it. I should be an alien anywhere else."

So we stayed. . . . And why did I never think of hot ginger tea mixed with honey? She takes better care of him than I did. But does she love him as much? I believe she loves him to the fullness of her heart, but it is a little heart—a cupful of love fills it to the brim. Is it enough for him? Perhaps it is. I have no way of knowing. She prattles on.

"The chrysanthemums are bright and healthy this autumn. They bloom against the northern wall of the big courtyard."

That is where they always bloomed. And I planted pink ones and white ones against the wall of the small courtyard outside our bedroom, but she does not mention those.

"He is working very hard just now. There are new classes and many new students. He works too hard. At night He cannot sleep. If He sleeps He mutters words I cannot understand."

Does he ever speak my name? If he does perhaps it would be too much to think that she would tell me. He is far away from me now. If we met I think he would still be far away. There are all these days between us in which I have no share. He would not be able to speak of them. I could not ask him about them and all the more because there was never reticence between us when we were together.

I fold the letters away. There is no time for all this

thinking. Rennie comes home tonight. I have his room ready, the walls are pale yellow, the furniture is polished and dustless, his bed is made fresh, there are red berries in a bowl on the chimney piece and wood is piled in the wide old-fashioned fireplace. Snow fell again in the night and he will want to ski and so I have waxed his skis and put them in the kitchen entry, waiting. Of course I finished everything too early and time plodded, the clock did not move. I toyed with the thought of putting up the Christmas tree and then knew I must not, for he and I have kept to the custom of my childhood when my father and I went up the hill beyond the sugar bush and cut the tree on Christmas Eve. It is important now to cling to family customs. They link the present with the past and reach into the future. If Gerald's mother had been able to draw her family into Baba's house and so have given Gerald a place in the history of the clan he would not have grown up solitary. But Baba perhaps would not allow it, or she perhaps felt herself cut off by her strange marriage and so she became a revolutionist. Revolutions are made only by those who are desolate and desperate. Now that is what I must somehow prevent Rennie from becoming. He must find his place here in the valley where my forebears lie buried. He must somhow belong to my country, or he will become a rebel wherever he goes.

I am growing too intense again. It is the strength and weakness of being mother to a son. A daughter, I think, would be always near me, within the reach of my words. But Rennie has already made his distance from me. He comes back a stranger. I must acquaint myself anew, as though we had not met before. I hope I have that wisdom.

So the anticipated evening draws near. The mountains cut off the final sunset but the sky is red above the snow. Baba feels the excitement in the house and tonight he refused to go to bed early. He asked for his best Chinese gown, a dark maroon satin with gold buttons, and he sits there in his chair by the window of his bedroom, his dragon-headed cane in his hand. The cane is not really comfortable for him to hold, and he uses a smooth malacca every day, but tonight he remembered the dragon-headed one and I had to search for it in the closet. His white hair and long white beard make him look like an ancient Chinese patriarch, for his skin, always dark, is now leather-hued and wrinkled. Only his proud old aquiline profile declares him Scotch and not Chinese in his ancestry.

As for me, I made the pretense of last things to be done to the supper table and I came downstairs to be near the front door. I have tied a branch of mountain pine and a clump of scarlet wintergreen berries to the brass knocker. I want Rennie to come in by the front door, and I station myself here.

Through the twilight I see at last the twin glow of automobile lights. It is he. I suppose he has hired a car at the station in Manchester. He did not tell me when he was coming and so I could not meet him. The car is here. I am suddenly faint and must lean my head against the door. Then I hear the knocker thunder against the brass plate beneath it. Perhaps it is not Rennie after all. Perhaps it is one of our rare passers-by. The door is unlocked and I tug at it, and then suddenly it is pushed in and there stand two tall men. One of them is Rennie, and the other is Sam, and it is Sam who speaks first.

141

"Hello, Mrs. MacLeod! I thought I'd come along with Rennie and see how my old gentleman is. You can throw me out if you don't want me for Christmas."

He shakes my hand enough to break my wrist, and his blue eyes twinkle and glow. He throws his arms across my shoulders and kisses me soundly on my cheek. And all this time, while I am stammering some sort of welcome, I see only Rennie, standing there waiting, a slight tall dark young man, smiling, and saying not a word. It occurs to Sam that he has been boisterous, for he steps back.

"Excuse me, ma'am."

And Rennie comes forward and takes my hand in both his, and he stoops and kisses me on the other cheek, so lightly that I scarcely feel the touch of his fresh cool lips.

"Hello, Mother—"

He looks down at me, I look up at him. He is not saying anything more now. I hasten to speak.

"Come in—come in. It's cold tonight. Come in where it's warm. Good skiing weather tomorrow, Rennie!"

They come in and Rennie stands looking around the hall and into the living room. I have lit all the lamps and I have lit the candles on the dining-room table. The table is set with my best linen and my mother's old silver. I have put a bowl of holly on the table. We cannot grow holly here, and I bought it at a dear price at the florist's shop in town.

"Does it look the same to you?" I ask Rennie.

He shakes his head and does not reply. No, it does not look the same to him because he is not the same. He is changed. And I discern in him a heartbreaking fear of me, his mother. He is afraid that I will try to

142

make him what he was before, a boy and not a man. He is not willing even to be my son if he has to be a boy again. I understand this in a flash of pain.

"Would you like to go to your rooms?" I asked very formally. "Rennie, your room is ready, and I have only to put some towels in the guest room for you, Sam. I'm glad you came."

Yes, I am glad. When I first saw him I was almost angry that a stranger had come with my son. But I know why he came. Rennie wanted him to come so that he would not be alone with me, his mother. He needs a man to keep him safe from me. I must be very cool and calm. I must make no demands on this tall silent young man. So I am glad that Sam has come. It will be easier to treat them both as strangers.

"You know your room, Rennie," I said cheerfully. "And, Sam, if you will turn here to the right—"

"How is the old gentleman?" Sam asked briskly.

"He'll be delighted to see you," I said, and hoped that Baba would remember him.

"Where is he?"

"Here." I opened the door of Baba's room, and Sam went in but I saw Rennie pass by and go into his own room and shut the door.

"Well, well," Sam shouted. He descended upon Baba and shook his hand while Baba stared at him helplessly.

"Sitting here looking like an old Emperor of China," Sam bellowed amiably. "How are you, Doctor Mac-Leod?"

He drew up a wooden chair in front of Baba and sat on it facing the back, his sandy hair on end and every tooth showing in his grin.

"I am well," Baba said cautiously. He looked at me,

appealing, and then at Sam. "Are you my grandson?" he inquired gently.

Sam roared. "Not quite—not quite! Rennie hasn't changed that much. Don't you remember me, sir? I fetched you to the shack on my ranch. Don't you remember? Why, you and me were wonderful friends!"

Baba remembered slowly. He nodded his head. He tapped his dragon-headed cane softly two or three times on the carpet.

"Sam," he said cautiously. "It's Sam."

"Right," Sam cried with delight. "Why, you're in fine shape. You've been taken real good care of—"

I longed to leave them and slip away to Rennie's room. If I were alone with my son surely there would be one good moment of embrace, just one, and I would ask no more. But Sam was watching me. When I stole toward the door he stopped me.

"Ma'am," he said, "you won't misunderstand me when I say it's better to leave Rennie to himself for a while. He'll come back to you in good time but it'll have to be his time."

"I feel it," I said, and sat down and waited.

And Rennie's door opened at last and he came in. He had changed his clothes to brown slacks and a tweed jacket that I had never seen before. His black hair was brushed smooth and he wore a red tie. I saw him as a man, a very handsome man. . . . Though young, he has reserves of power somewhere. Shall I ever know him again and if so, then how?

"How are you, Grandfather?" he said and he came to Baba and knelt at his side as a Chinese grandson might have done and took Baba's hand.

Baba stared at him reflectively.

"Are you my son Gerald?" he asked.

"Only your grandson," Rennie said.

They looked at each other and, face to face, I saw the resemblance between them for the first time. Rennie's profile, changing with manhood, takes on the Scotch lines and not the Chinese.

"My grandson," Baba repeated, and suddenly he leaned forward and kissed Rennie on the forehead. I had never seen him kiss anyone before. Rennie was moved, and put Baba's hand to his cheek.

"I'm glad I came home," he said. He turned to me and I saw tears in his eyes.

We had a merry evening after that. Those two young men made a chair of their crossed hands and they carried Baba downstairs and he sat at the table with us. Then, for gaiety, I ran upstairs and put on my wine velvet dinner gown, which I had not worn since Gerald and I parted. The last night in Shanghai we went alone to dine at the Astor Hotel and afterwards to dance, and I put on this one festive gown that I had saved through all the war. We danced cheek to cheek, forgetting the crowded streets outside, and determined for a few hours to mingle with the European guests gathered in the hotel, most of them ready to sail away forever from the country they loved but to which they could never belong. And we knew, Gerald and I, without ever saying it, that he would stay and I must go. I am sure he knew.

For a moment tonight I was about to take the gown off again, and then I would not. Everything I was and owned must become a part of this house, this valley, and I have no other country than my own. So I went downstairs, and the two young men stood up when I came in and each of them looked at me with surprise. I was suddenly a woman, and they had not realized it

before. Well, I was glad that Rennie saw me as someone else than mother, for perhaps he will not fear me
so much. As for Sam, it does not matter what he saw.

I put Rennie at the head of the table, and I sat at
the foot, with Baba at my right so that I could cut his
meat for him. The soup was hot in the Chinese bowls
I had once bought in New York because they were
like the ones I had in Peking, only the ware is not so
fine, and so we began our evening meal. And Rennie
was suddenly quite gay, too, and he began to talk, and
Sam was as suddenly silent and almost shy.

"I'm going to teach Sam to ski," Rennie said. "He's
lived in such flat country that he doesn't know what
it is to ski down a mountainside."

"There are extra skis in the attic," I said.

"I don't know as I want to come down a mountain,"
Sam said. "It takes nerve, the kind I haven't."

"Of all the kinds of nerve you have," Rennie said,
"you should be able to summon another. I've seen
you come down out of the sky in that single-engine
plane of yours at a speed that ought to make you
ready to ski down Everest itself."

"I don't carry the engine on my feet," Sam said.

They were hungry and they ate heartily and I sat
and watched them. It was good to have guests at the
table. I had sat alone so long. I took pride in the roast
lamb and the peas and the small browned potatoes
and lettuce salad. And I had remembered the apple
pies that Rennie loves, served with cheese slices and
hot coffee.

"I don't remember your being such a good cook,"
Rennie said, throwing me a smile.

"This is a special effort," I said.

"I wouldn't like to have to eat as good a dinner

146

every day," Rennie declared. He had recovered from whatever shyness he had and was himself again. I saw him let out his belt a notch or two, hiding this from me politely. Rennie's good manners are as natural to him as breathing. He absorbed them in Peking from the most mannerly people in the world, and though he tried to be rough and rude when he left China, he was old enough now to dare to be himself, or very nearly. He was still cautious with me.

When dinner was over the knocker clanged again. We had left the table, I forbidding any help with clearing. Time enough for that later, I told Sam, who began at once to stack dishes. Baba was lifted into the living room and put in a chair by the fire, and I had sat opposite him, and Rennie and Sam had pulled up the yellow satin sofa facing the chimney piece when we heard the clangor.

Rennie turned to me. "Do you expect someone?"

"No," I said. "I cannot imagine who would come at this hour."

He went into the hall and opened the door and Bruce Spaulden stood there, holding in his hand a bunch of pink roses wrapped in cellophane. Rennie stared at him. They knew each other, for Bruce had brought Rennie through tonsillitis, but they stared as though at strangers.

"No one is ill here," Rennie said.

"Rennie!" I cried. "For heaven's sake—"

I went to the door myself and Bruce held out the roses and I took them.

"Come in," I said. "We are sitting around the fire."

He came in and Rennie stood watchful and silent. I put the roses in an old gray pottery bowl that had stood on the table since I was a child. Before I sat down I saw that Baba had fallen peacefully asleep, his head thrown back and his eyes closed.

"Ought we to take him upstairs?" I asked Bruce.

"He looks comfortable," Bruce said, "and he couldn't be more soundly asleep."

We sat down and Rennie was silent between the two men and I caught him looking at me strangely now and again. I felt suddenly happy as I had not been for a long time and soon we were all talking, and Bruce got up and went to the pantry and made some hot coffee, for he will not drink anything else, but Rennie fetched the wine that I keep in the house and poured out glasses for himself and Sam, and I wanted nothing and so we sat down again and the talk flowed triangularly between the two men and me. Rennie sat silent and watching.

I really belong here, I kept thinking. It is here I was born, and if I were not so lonely, I could forget Peking and at last perhaps I could even forget Gerald. I have not laughed for a long time but I found myself laughing, laughing at the three men. Each in his way was playing for my attention, Sam very brusque and western and masculine and Bruce dark and caustic and wary, and Rennie the young man standing aside from the fencing between the two older men, but watchful and tending the fire. The talk ranged but it was all for my ears, the fencers preening and displaying themselves before my eyes. I felt a tenderness, amused, unspecified, but valid.

"Revolution," Sam declared, "is an inevitable process. We do not grow by accumulation, as barnacles do. We burst our skins, like snakes, we cast off the old encasements, and emerge afresh."

I was amazed to hear him speak without a trace

of his harsh western idiom. The ranchman's drawl was a shield. I had never seen the real man before.

Bruce drew upon his pipe, slowly and deeply. Twin jets of smoke feathered from his thin nostrils. "There never was a revolution in man's history that paid its way. The end is always lost in the conflict and confusion out of which evil men rise to power."

"You can't hold back revolution for all of that," Sam insisted. "Endurance has its limit. Explosion is inevitable. Look at China—"

He turned to me and the winds of Asia rushed into the warm closed room. I was swept across the sea again. By force of will I refused to go.

"Let us not talk of China," I said. "Let us never talk of China. Who knows what is happening there?"

Rennie looked up from the fire and the iron poker dropped from his hands. His eyes met mine. I knew I should have to tell him.

The life went out of the evening. I could not listen now to the argument between the men. They continued, their eyes covertly upon me, demanding attention which I could not give. . . . How can I tell Rennie about his father?

. . . "Come into my room, Rennie," I said when the evening was over. I was casual, I made my voice cheerful. "You and I have had no chance to talk. Let's light the fire and settle ourselves."

We had said good night to Bruce at the front door and then to Sam at the head of the stairs. Bruce held my hand for a moment, and I could not be warm. "Thank you for the pink roses," I said stupidly.

"When I think of roses I think of you," he said under his breath. That was much for him to say but I could

149

not muster a smile in reply. My heart was already hammering in my breast. How can I tell Rennie so that he will not hate his father?

"Sit down, Rennie," I said.

I sat in the old red velvet armchair that had once belonged to my Boston grandmother. He sat down in the wooden Windsor opposite me. He had lit the fire in my room and the logs were dry and already blazing.

"I can't get used to the way you look," I said. Indeed I cannot. His face has lost his boyish roundness. The cheekbones are defined, the jaw is firm. I should be hard put to it to say where Rennie came from, were he a stranger to me. Spain? Italy? Brazil? North India? Yet he is my own son.

"Tell me what you like best at college," I said.

"Math. Math and music."

I have forgotten to say that Rennie has always loved music. This perhaps is my gift to him. Many hours of my own youth I spent at the old square piano downstairs in the parlor, but since I came home I have not been able to play. I have not even given Rennie lessons as I might have. Living on the brink of final separation from Gerald I have not been able to endure music. Yet I have never forbidden it to Rennie and he has played when he wished.

"It's a good combination, Rennie—the combination Confucius required for the civilized man. The superior man, the gentleman, must know the disciplines of mathematics and music."

"They are allied," Rennie said. "They demand the same precision and abstraction."

I am awed by his growth in mind as well as in body. "Shall you go into music for livelihood?" I inquired.

"I want to be a scientist. Science combines the abstract and the precise."

"Your father will be pleased."

To this Rennie did not reply. He never replies when I mention his father.

"And what about George Bowen's sister?" I inquired, half-playfully. Now this would never do. I was avoiding the opportunity of his silence. I did not care about George Bowen's sister.

Rennie did not look at me. His eyes were fixed upon the fire. "What about her?"

"Well, is she pretty?"

"She is not pretty—she's beautiful."

"Dark or fair? Short or tall?"

"Tall, fair, and calm."

"Not like me—"

He cast a quick glance at me, measuring, comparing, and looked again at the fire. "No."

"Do you like her very much, Rennie?"

"I don't know. I don't want to know, I suppose. I'd rather not be hurt again."

"There's plenty of time," I said.

"Yes."

Here fell the next silence, and I would not let myself be a coward about it.

"Rennie, I want to talk about your father."

He lifted his head at this, reluctantly interested.

"Have you had a letter?"

"Not recently—not from him. But I did have a—a special letter."

"Why didn't you tell me when it came?"

"You were too young," I said. "You wouldn't have understood. You'd have blamed him."

"What has he done?"

151

"Wait," I said. "I must explain."

And so I began at the beginning. I told him how we met, Gerald and I. I told him how we fell in love. I couldn't tell him of our first night together. That belongs to Gerald and to me, a treasure locked in memory. I told him of Peking and how in those years the love we had begun here in this narrow Vermont valley deepened and widened into a life complete in companionship.

"There are a few such marriages, Rennie," I said. "My mother told me I could never be happy with Gerald but she was wrong. I was happy and so was he. We delighted each in the other. The ancestors did not matter. Well, the truth is that perhaps they mattered very much. They added their peculiar and fascinating variety. I remember your father and I talked about them sometimes. I remember your father said once that our marriage was all the more complete because the responsibility for it rested solely on ourselves. Our ancestors would not have approved."

Rennie is too quick for me. "What is it that you really want to say?"

"I want to tell you first that what has happened is not the fault of your father nor is it mine. If the world had not split apart under our feet, we would still be living in the house in Peking and not here."

"And why aren't we?" he demanded.

"You know," I said. "You know and you needn't ask. It is because of me. It is because I am American, and because your father is half-American. And there is no fault in either of us for that. It is the split in the world that has driven us apart, exactly as though a tidal wave had rushed between us on a beach and swept us in opposite directions."

"He could have left China," Rennie said.

"He could not."

"And why not?" Rennie insisted. I saw by his bitter face that he was angry with his father.

"I defend your father," I said. "He is not here to speak for himself. And besides, if you must blame anyone, blame Baba. He married your Chinese grandmother without loving her, and that was the primary sin."

With this I got up and I fetched the picture of his grandmother and I told him about her and how the story of Han Ai-lan was imbedded in the story of her country and in the times in which we live.

"She who knew she was not loved by her husband gave her life instead to her country and to what she thought was her duty. And her son—your father, Rennie—ate the sour fruit and your teeth, Rennie, are set on edge."

"Did she love Baba?" Rennie's voice was low.

"I am sure she did, for if she had not she could never have given herself so utterly elsewhere. She did not expect to love him but she did love him, and was rejected by him. There is nothing so explosive in this world as love rejected."

"My father has rejected you," Rennie said brutally.

I denied this and passionately. "He has not rejected me. He cannot reject me as long as we love each other. Love still works in us its mercies."

He saw me now, I believe, as someone else than his mother. He saw me as a woman in love, and he could not reply. He has never seen a woman in love and his eyes fell before mine.

"It is time for me to show you the letter," I said. I rose and I opened the locked box and took out the sealed letter and gave it to him. He broke the seal and opened the letter and read it. I sat in my chair and waited. He read it twice, thoughtfully. Then he folded it and put it back into the envelope and placed it on the small table beside him.

"Thank you, Mother," he said.

"I have given permission to the Chinese woman," I said. "I have said that I understand. I have said that I want him to be comforted in his house. . . . So I will also show you her letters."

Now I opened the drawer of my rosewood desk and gave him the letters from Mei-lan. He read them, his face impassive. He read them quickly and folded them and handed them back to me.

"She has nothing to do with me," he said. "And I cannot understand why he has let her come into our house."

His voice was so hard that I could not bear it. "We do not know how much he was compelled, once he had made his choice to stay in Peking."

"Ah," Rennie said, "I still ask, why did he make that choice if he loved us? I shall keep on asking. For me there is no answer."

"You do not love your father enough to forgive him," I said.

"Perhaps that is true," Rennie agreed.

He got up suddenly and walked to the window and stood there looking out into the night. The light of the lamp shone through the glass upon the falling snow. The fire burned suddenly blue and a log fell into the ash.

He turned to face me. "Mother, I have something to tell you, too. All that business of Allegra—it very nearly drove me back to Peking. If I am to be rejected because my grandmother was Chinese, I thought, I'd better go back to China. But I'll never go back now. I'll stay with you. This shall be my country. I will have no other."

I cried out, "Oh, Rennie, Rennie, don't decide so quickly. Don't decide against your father!"

"I am not deciding against him. I am deciding for you," Rennie said. And he stooped and kissed my cheek and went away.

I shall not follow him. I know my son. The decision has not come quickly. He has been tortured by indecision, he has been torn between his two countries, between his father and me. And he has chosen me and mine. Oh, Gerald, forgive me I pray that you will have other sons. Indeed I do so pray. If I have robbed you of the son that is ours, can I help myself? It is Rennie who decides his own life. And he has as much right to decide as I had when I followed you to Peking and as you had when you would not come home with me. Yes, this is home at last, this Vermont valley, these mountains, the house of my fathers.

When Rennie left me I sat a long time before the dying fire, a weight gone from me. I am no longer alone in my own country. My son is with me. I shall be happy again, some day.

. . . Even yet there has been no thought of cutting myself off from Gerald. Months have passed after that gay Christmas day. Rennie is nearing the end of his college year. Sam has been twice to see me. He urges me to divorce Gerald, and today he flew in from New York only for an hour, he said, not knowing how this day would end. For it is night and he is here. We have telegraphed for Rennie to come at once, because of what has happened. It was this morning, and Sam was arguing with me, impatient, angry, insistent.

"You must divorce that fellow in Peking—he's no husband to you, Elizabeth!"

"I shall never divorce Gerald," I said. "Indeed, I have no cause. He loves me."

"If you call desertion love," Sam bellowed.

"He has not deserted me." I was shouting, too.

"If it is not desertion, I do not know what to call it," Sam roared.

Of course he does not know the whole story. He surmises, because there is no talk of Gerald himself— and me. I tried to explain without telling anything.

"Gerald has not deserted me nor I him. We are divided by history, past and present."

"His father is American," Sam said stubbornly. "He could have come home with you."

"Ah, but you see this is not home to him!"

"Baloney," Sam said crossly. "He's no fool. He could adapt himself. He could have got a job in some university here as well as in Peking."

"Home is a matter of the heart and the spirit. His would have died here," I said.

"You're still in love with him," Sam said, and he turned on me so fierce a stare that I could not defend myself.

"Can't you see that I am determined to marry you?" he cried.

"Oh, no, Sam—no—no!"

"Yes!"

We were both breathless, both glaring at each other. Sam bent over me and I pushed him away.

"Don't—"

"Do you hate me?"

"No—not hate—"

At this moment we heard Baba fall in the room above. The beams of the living room are not ceiled. We heard the clatter of Baba's cane and then so light a fall, his old bones all but fleshless, that we might scarcely have heard except for the terrible wrenching groan. I ran upstairs, Sam following me, and there Baba lay. I do not know whether he had heard us. We never know what he hears and we were talking more loudly than we knew. Perhaps Baba had got out of his chair with some thought of coming downstairs, although he has not walked alone across the room since Christmas. He lay there. His head had struck the stone hearth of the fireplace. He was dead.

. . . We have come home from Baba's funeral. Sam stayed, he and Bruce Spaulden took care of every detail for me. Had it been possible, I would have sent Baba's ashes to Peking and to Gerald. Well, I suppose it would have been possible. It has been done for others who have died here or in England, exiles so deeply divided from their own peoples and lands, so enamored of another culture, that they could think of no other burial place upon the globe than in Peking. Then I reflected that Baba had left Peking of his own desire, and even his ashes would not be welcome there now, for he belonged to the old China, the China of Confucius and of emperors.

"Let us keep Baba here with us," I told Rennie.

"Yes," Rennie said. "Let us keep him."

He arrived barely in time for the funeral, and not alone. He brought with him a tall fair girl, a calm quiet girl whose every movement is slow grace.

"This is Mary Bowen," Rennie said.

"Strange, I have never heard your name," I said, and suddenly I wanted to kiss her. I leaned forward and put my lips to her smooth young cheek.

"You look like a Mary," I said.

"I'm a pretty good Martha, too," she said and smiled.

"Then Rennie is in luck," I said, "for it is not every woman who is both."

They were in love. I could see that they were in love. I know the signs, how well, and I was comforted. I took their hands and between them I went upstairs to where Baba lay in his blue Chinese robe. He lay on top of the white counterpane, and I had put on his feet his black velvet Chinese shoes. Jim Standman, the undertaker, when he had finished his private task, let me help with the rest, for I did not want Baba taken away and so in his own room we made him ready. Under his hands crossed upon his breast I had put his little worn copy of The Book of Changes.

Mary stepped forward alone as we entered the bedroom. She stood looking at him.

"How beautiful he is," she whispered. She turned to Rennie. "You didn't tell me he looked like this."

"He is beautiful," I said, "and somehow more beautiful now than he was alive."

"I wish I could have heard his voice speaking," she said.

And then she went to Rennie, and she lifted his hand and held it against her cheek. From that moment I loved her as my own daughter.

. . . This afternoon a few neighbors gathered with us under the pine tree on the mountain behind the house and there we buried Baba. Matt helped to dig the grave this morning and we lined it with pine branches, while Mrs. Matt made the collation for the

funeral feast. She boiled a ham, for she thinks a baked
ham is not worth eating, and set out sandwiches and
cake and tea and coffee, ready for the return from
the grave. The day was quiet and the sky mildly over-
cast, and the minister, a retired clergyman from Manchester who tends our spiritual life here in the valley
when we feel the need, read certain passages from the
New Testament, which I had marked because Baba
had once declared to me that they were taken origi-
nally from the wisdom of Asia and perhaps from Confucius himself, "for," said Baba, "it is not accident that
Jesus uttered the very words long ago spoken by
Confucius and Buddha. He was in Nepal in his youth,
if we are to believe folk rumors."

I had listened when he said this, paying little heed,
for Baba believed wholeheartedly that man and his
wisdom began in the East, and I was used to such talk.
Now the good words fell gently and with deep mercy
upon the quiet air, and to the ears of the listening
Christians they brought no doubts, though Baba and
I had our secret. The voice was the voice of Jesus
whom the Vermonters call God, but the words are the
words of older gods. Oh, I am full of such secrets,
but I shall not tell them. I will carry them into my
grave with me, too, for to speak them here would be
to raise only doubts and controversy. I live in a narrow valley but it is my home.

After the ceremony was over, and we did not weep,
neither Rennie nor I, for death is not sad at the end
of a long life, we came home again. Mrs. Matt was
bustling about in a black silk dress and a huge white
apron and we sat in the living room with the guests.
We ate and drank and spoke quietly, not of Baba, for
indeed few of the neighbors knew him except as a

frail and exquisite ghost. No, we talked of the valley gossip, of whether the summer would be late, of how scanty the sugar crop was this year, the winter lingering too long and then spring breaking too quickly. In a little while they were all gone. Bruce stopped a moment with me to search my face and tell me that I looked pale and must rest.

"You won't mourn?" he said.

"Not for Baba," I said.

"You must not mourn for anyone," he said urgently.

I could not tell him, not yet, that with Baba's death died also the symbol of the past. Baba was a link with other years and with a beloved city, with a house which I had believed my home. But Bruce's concern was comforting and when I smiled, I saw that he longed to kiss me. Longing smoldered in his gray eyes and yearning in his controlled Vermont face. I was not ready. I could not bear the touch of another man's lips—not yet.

So the day ended, and Sam went away, too. I think he saw Bruce's face. He was standing there in the hall behind us, and I heard his footstep, abrupt and unconcealed, when he turned and went into the living room. He left soon after that, saying that he must get to New York by morning to see about a contract with some dealer there, a horse trainer for a circus, he said, who wanted six young palomino colts, exactly matched, which he had been collecting on the ranch, though it was the first time I have ever heard of circuses and matched palomino colts. He shook my hand hard and stared at me. "Let me know if you want anything," he said. "I'm on call."

Suddenly, without permission, he bent and kissed me on the lips and I stepped back and nearly fell.

"You don't like it," he muttered.

"No," I said honestly.

"I won't do it again," he said and went away. I am sorry he was hurt but I do not like to be kissed when I am not ready. The days of my youth are past and to a woman full grown a kiss means everything—or nothing.

All this took place on the very day of Baba's funeral and I was glad for that day's end. In the evening Rennie and Mary and I were quietly together on the terrace, for I wanted to be out of the house and the air was unusually mild even for May. These two must go away again tomorrow, and then I shall be alone. It worried them both that I was to be alone, and I did not know how to make them believe that I did not mind, for indeed I do not know whether I shall mind being alone in this great old house. I have no near neighbors and the forest in the valley changes strangely with the night. When the afternoon sun slants through the near trees to lie upon the beds of fern and brake, the forest is lively with light and color, harmless enough, surely, and not to be feared. But when the mountain intervenes between house and sky then darkness falls swiftly, and the forest loses its kindliness. Staring into shadows growing sinister with night, I remember that for thirty miles and more forest mingles with swamp and quicksands, wherein hunters have been lost and never found. Once a woman, a botanist, was lost in the forest that surrounds my home. Therefore I do not know whether I can live here alone. It may be that the darkness of the nights will encircle me too deeply.

"I wish I were finished with college," Rennie said.

"I wish that Mary and I were married and living here with you."

It is the first word that he had spoken to me of marriage.

"If you two are to be married, then I shall be so happy that I shall have no time to be afraid," I replied.

For even in a few hours I can see that Mary is the one I would choose for Rennie. If he had returned to his father's country, then no, I would not have thought it possible for Mary to have gone with him to Peking. Mind you, it can be done. There are other American women still there, but I do not know how they can be happy when they hear their country reviled and must be silent. Mind you again, I know that the plain people in villages and towns do not believe the evil they hear about us. The Chinese are very old and wise as a folk, and they are able to hold their peace for a hundred years and more if they must, until the times roll round again. The life of no human being is as long as they can hold their peace. I cannot therefore wish for a woman like myself to give herself away to such a country, or to such a people, for they are so easy to love that once loved they can never be forgotten, and what cannot be forgotten one day divides and then choice and decision are compelled. I believe if Gerald's other country had not been China he could not have forsaken me. But that country and especially that city, the city of Peking, are invincible in love. Any woman could be defeated by them.

"We shall certainly be married," Mary said.

"The question is when," Rennie added.

"Why should there be any question?" I inquired. "If you want to be married, then marry."

Here I remembered Allegra. "Unless Mary's family

has some reason of their own for delay—perhaps because you are so young, Mary."

"I have no family except my twin brother George," Mary said. "Our parents died when we were children and we lived with my grandmother. Now she is dead, too."

It is interesting to discover how secretly wicked one's self can be. For the sake of my son I rejoiced that three innocent people were in their graves. I was ashamed enough not to say I was glad and yet honest enough not to say I was sorry.

"You may marry when you like then," I said. "The wedding can be here in this house where I was married to Rennie's father and that will make me happy. I shall not mind living alone if I know you are married."

"Thank you, Mother," Rennie said. He was lying full length upon the long terrace chair, and he got up and went to Mary's side, for I was between them in the round-backed log chair, and he stood before her and took her hand.

"Will you marry me on the eighteenth of June, when I shall be twenty years old?"

"I will," she said, and smiled up at him.

The moonlight shone on her long fair hair and on Rennie's face. I thought them the most beautiful pair in the world, and my heart yearned for Gerald who could not see them. I used once to be able to reach him with my concentrated thought, but for a long time I had not done so. Now I tried again. I gathered my whole energy and will and intention upon him, far away in Peking. At this hour he would perhaps be sitting in the court outside the living room. Were I there it is where we would be, for in the month of

May the lilacs are very fine in the court, the heavy-scented deeply purple Chinese lilacs and the white lilacs which are at once more hardy, more prolific and yet more delicate than the lilacs are here. I tried to reach him and let him share what I saw, this beautiful cream-skinned man who is our son, and Mary, tall and fair and calm. . . . I could not reach him. Again my heart, my mind, were stopped by a barrier I do not understand and beyond it I could not go. . . .

"On the eighteenth day of June this house will be ready for you," I promised Rennie and Mary.

When I went upstairs to bed an hour later, leaving them alone together on the terrace, even the ghost of Baba was gone. There was no smell of death in the house, and I could scarcely remember his funeral, or see the new-made grave under the pines. Perhaps the real Baba was never here, or Baba was only the shell that was left of the stately gentleman and scholar who had once been Dr. MacLeod. All that had been was no more. I could almost imagine now that even Gerald was gone, or that he had never been, except that he had given me my son.

. . . I am not what is called psychic. I am far too earthy a woman for that. Gerald said once that I am incurably domestic, and it is true that I am. I can be absorbed in the everyday happenings in house and garden and easily diverted at any time by the talk and antics of human beings. I am not an intellectual, in spite of a Phi Beta Kappa key won in my senior year at college, at which no one was more shocked than I, for I knew even then that I did not deserve this insignia of the learned. Nor am I a dreamer of dreams and I have never seen visions.

I make this statement, this affirmation, because I swear that last night, at a quarter past two, I saw Gerald here in my room. It is true that I am alone in the house and have been alone now for five weeks, ever since Rennie and Mary left me the morning after Baba's funeral. I have had, however, an unusual number of valley visitors. Matt comes early and stays late, and Mrs. Matt makes the pretext of bringing his lunch the occasion for "running in," as she calls it, to see how I am doing. She always stays and always talks, mainly about Matt and his cantankerous ways. Mrs. Matt is an ignorant woman who will not learn that life and man do not change, and that it is the woman who must bend if she is not to break. I know all of Matt's faults by now, even to the obnoxious wheeze of his snores and that he will not put his false teeth properly in a glass of water at night but leaves them to grin at her from the bedside table.

The minister, too, comes to see me, and so does Mrs. Monroe, the teacher in our valley's one-room school. And Bruce Spaulden has been here twice, never to stay, merely to drop in at breakfast time before he makes his calls, to observe me, he says, and make sure that I am not what he describes as "moping."

"Are you happy?" he asked me only yesterday. I was weeding the strawberry beds in the warm corner between the main house and the ell, the only place where strawberry plants do not frost-kill, although even here they must be mulched with manure and straw over the winter.

"I am neither happy nor unhappy," I told him. "I am in a state of blessed calm."

"Permanently so?" he asked, tilting his black eyebrows at me.

"Probably not," I said. "Probably it is a transition state between past and future. I don't know. I merely enjoy my ignorance."

"Not too lonely?"

"How can I be with a wedding in the house in June?"

There was nothing unusual in yesterday. I did such work in the house as was needful and it is very little. One person cannot dirty floors and tables and what I eat scarcely disturbs the kitchen. Even my bed is quickly made, for I am a quiet sleeper. Gerald turned and tossed, but I on my side of the wide Chinese bed with the American mattress lay, he said, like a sleeping doll. Nevertheless I wake easily.

Last night I woke, as I usually do in the night. I like to know the time, and it is usually the same, almost to the minute. The radiant face of the bedside clock showed quarter past two. Ever since I was parted from Gerald I resolutely turn on the light and take up my book, whatever it is, and of late I have no taste for stories or for poetry. When I put Rennie's room in order after he left, I looked through his bookcase and found a thin small book whose title proclaimed it a simple and shortened exposition of the meaning of Einstein's theory of relativity, "for Simple Readers," the subtitle said. That surely am I, and I brought the book back to my own room. Simple as it declared itself, the book has so far confounded me. I am even more simple. I do not easily comprehend large abstract matters. I read the book faithfully, nevertheless, all but spelling the sentences over and over in my nightly efforts to understand them. I say this to prove that I am really not in the least psychic nor even very imaginative. I have a good practical brain and an excellent memory and this is as far as I go.

After the fourth reading of the book, however, I suddenly understood the fundamental relationship between matter and energy. Oh, I muttered aloud—for I am ashamed to say that I am beginning to talk to myself sometimes, but only in the night when the house is altogether silent, except for creaking beams and crying wind—oh, but this is fascinating, this is exciting. The essence of matter is transmutable into energy. I can see that.

The comprehension came to me suddenly only night before last, and immediately I felt myself possessed by a strange soft peace. Mind and body relaxed and fell into sleep. When I awakened it was late morning, and the sun was streaming across the room. I rose quickly, and as I have said, the day was busy with small affairs. Mrs. Matt stayed too long, and night fell before I had finished the plans I had made for the day. For I have learned that if my life is to have meaning as a whole, now that Gerald and I are apart and Rennie is a man, then each day must have its individual order, so that when night falls I can say that I have done what I planned for the day, and the sum total of days makes a year and years make a life.

Well, then, I was tired last night, and mildly discontented with myself because I had not completed the day. I did not open the book but went immediately to sleep. When I woke at quarter past two, as I have said, my mind was clear and I was eager to read again in the light of fresh comprehension. I had only opened the book when I knew that I was not alone. I was not frightened, only filled with involuntary wonder. For I looked up and I saw Gerald, standing just inside the closed door. He was sad and thin and much older. He had a short beard, his hair was cropped very short, and he wore Chinese clothes, not the robes of a gentleman but a uniform of the sort that students used to wear, made of dark stuff and the jacket buttoned to the throat. I could not see his form clearly, but his face was very clear. He smiled at me, his grave dark eyes suddenly bright. I think he put out his hand to me, but of this I am not sure for I leaped from my bed and I cried out to him.

"Gerald, Gerald, oh, darling—"

I was stopped by a frightful agony in his face, but only for one instant. Then I ran to hold him in my arms, but he was gone. I stood where I had seen him stand. There was no one here and the floor was cold beneath my bare feet. I crept back into bed shivering and afraid. I have seen Gerald. I have no doubt of it. And I have seen him as he is now. It could not be a dream nor a trick of memory, else I would have seen him as he had been when we parted, his face as it looked when he stood on the dock at Shanghai, when we gazed at each other until the river mists crept between us and my ship sailed out to sea.

"I feel as though my very flesh was torn from yours," he had written me.

Now he was bearded, his hair was cut short, he wore the uniform he had always hated, even when his students put it on proudly. A prisoner's uniform, he had called it, lacking style and grace and always dingy blue or muddy gray. I had never seen him as I saw him now. Therefore it was no dream. I have seen matter transmuted into energy in his shape and form.

It was impossible to sleep after that. I dressed and went downstairs and walked about the house until the pale dawn gleamed behind the mountains. I do not know what a vision means. Does it signify life or death? I have no way of knowing. And why was his last look an agony? How shall I ever know?

. . . I am surprised that I am not in the least frightened because I have seen Gerald. I am overcome with sadness but not with fear. I cannot be afraid of Gerald in whatever form he comes to me, but I remember the stories I have always laughed at, the tales of dead people who appear to their loved ones, the ghosts and spirits in whom I have never believed. I still do not believe. I say to myself that there is some trick of sight and subconscious which betrays my common sense. Then I find myself leading to conversation on the subject of distant persons who suddenly appear before those who think of them, although I tell no one that I have seen Gerald. Mrs. Matt, for example, believes everything I doubt. She declares that she has seen three times the face of her mother, who lived and died in Ireland.

"Three times I have seen the blessed woman," she said today, "and each time was after she was dead."

I begged her to tell me what she saw.

"I saw my mother on her knees, a-prayin'," Mrs. Matt said solemnly. She was sitting at the kitchen table drinking a cup of stone-black tea while I finished my luncheon sandwich. "On her knees she was, her hand uplifted-like, and her hair streamin' down her back. She was cryin' while she prayed and she wore her old black dress but with no apron. Except on a Sunday she had always her apron on, and so I know it was a Sunday I saw her. Later I had the word that it was the very Sunday my father died, and I knew she saw him goin' down to hell. It was what he deserved but it was hard on her, bless her, and she cried."

"And the second time, Mrs. Matt?"

"The second time was when I had made up my mind to leave Matt. Yes, my dear," she said nodding her head at me. "I did so make up my mind. He'd had one of them jealous fits of his." She leaned close to me, her eyes on the kitchen door. Outside Matt was chopping wood.

"He wasn't the father of my first child," she whispered, "and he's never let me forget. Suspicious he is of every man—he's been my torment, that he has, these forty years."

I brushed aside the familiar complaint.

"And the third time, Mrs. Matt?"

She looked blank. "There was only the one time, dearie, and Matt married me before the blessed baby was born."

"The third time you saw your mother—"

"Ah yes, that! Well, the third time was on a bright Easter mornin'. I'd had a grand fight with Matt the night before and I was in no mood for church. To church I would not go and so I put on my old clothes and scrubbed the kitchen floor. Matt yelled at me to get up and come to church with him and the children —six of them we had by then, all small, and it was against the seventh that I'd fought him in the night. But I wouldn't go and he marched off, leaving me on my knees in a swirl of soap and water. When the house was quiet-like, I got up and put away my rag and pail and I washed myself and put on a clean nightygown and laid myself in a clean bed to sleep back my strength. It was then I saw my mother for the last time in resurrection. She was in white, like an angel, but her hair was down her back in a little gray pigtail as she always had it for the night. And she said to me, 'Poor soul, ye're only a woman, and ye must tak' it as best ye can.'

" 'True, Mother mine,' I said, and went off to sleep like a babe and when I woke, Matt was back and he'd fed the children and himself and I got up restored."

A foolish story, and Mrs. Matt is an ignorant and sometimes mischievous old woman but she believes what she saw.

In the afternoon I went to the small library in our nearest town and surprised our prim spinster librarian by finding half a dozen books on dreams and visions. I am half-ashamed of wanting to read them, for I am accustomed to my own skeptic views and I have no faith in second sight. It is Einstein who unsettles me. If a strong stout log of wood, a length of pure matter, can be transmuted into energy before my eyes, into ash and flame and heat, cannot a living body, a brilliant mind, a deep and spiritual soul, be transmuted into its own likeness but a different stuff? What impels me now is not the old wives' tales and the ghosts of the dead, for these my doubts are as valid as ever they have been. No, I am impelled by the infinite possibilities suggested to me by a gnarled little scientist whom I must respect because the world respects him. I have embarked upon a quest. I go in search of the one I love. Is Gerald living or is he dead?

. . . The quest ended today in a way so simple, so tragic, that I have no need of further search. A letter from Mei-lan, posted this time from Calcutta, tells me of Gerald's death. She is not in Calcutta. She is still in Peking, in the house there, awaiting, she tells me, the birth of her first child, Gerald's child. By some means she smuggled the letter out of China and into India. Perhaps a visiting delegation of Indian diplomats contained one who was Gerald's friend. To him perhaps she gave the letter to hide in his clothing until he could post it from another country.

The letter is short and written in haste. There are blots on the paper—tears perhaps. I will not repeat its words. I want to forget them and I shall destroy the letter. Its message is simply this: Gerald was shot while trying to escape from Peking. She did not know that he planned to escape.

"I think he longed to see you," she writes. "I think he dreamed to go somehow to India with the Indians."

He was always watched, of course. They never trusted him. I do not know whether among the servants there was one who betrayed him. He was not good at packing clothes or making practical arrangements. I always did such things for him. And it is possible that he did not trust even his Chinese wife.

"He did tell me nothing," she writes. "I think he wished no blame to fall on me. I can always say I do not know."

. . . Gerald was shot in the back through the left shoulder and just outside his own gate. He got no further than that. It was early afternoon, the sun was shining, he appeared to be returning to his classes at the university. The gateman stood in the open gate and he saw a man in the hateful uniform step from behind the corner. When Gerald came near, the man shot him with a pistol at close range. Then he disappeared. The gateman dared not shout. He lifted Gerald in his arms and brought him inside and laid him

172

on the stones of the main court. Then he locked the gate.

"We buried him secretly in the small court outside his bedroom," Mei-lan writes.

Early afternoon in Peking would perhaps be quarter past two here in our valley, quarter past two in the night. Dare I believe?

I do not know. I shall never know. All that I do know is that my beloved is no more. In this world, while I live, I shall not see his face again.

. . . I have taken up the routine of my days. There is no way to answer the letter, and so I have destroyed it. When I could write calmly, I wrote to Rennie that his father was dead.

"He had made up his mind, it seems, to come to us. That is what she believes, at least—his Chinese wife. He tried to live without us and he could not. Love was stronger in the end than country, stronger than history. This is our comfort. This is the message he sends us, by means of his death. It is enough for us to know. It is enough to make you forgive him, Rennie. Please forgive him! It will make life so much easier for me, so much more happy, if I know you have forgiven your father."

Here I paused to consider whether I should tell Rennie that I had seen Gerald clearly at the moment after he had died. His spirit escaping his body came home to me, to be visible for a moment, to be remembered forever. Then I decided that I would not tell Rennie. He would not believe, and perhaps I do not wish to test my own faith. It is not necessary. I can wait until it is time for me to know.

Rennie's reply was swift. "I do forgive him, Mother.

I forgive my father freely and with love, and of my own accord. I do this for my own sake. If it makes you happy, so much the better. And I have told Mary."

... There is no need for me to write any more upon these blank pages. What I have had to say has been said. The spring has slipped past and it is summer. I have busied myself in everyday matters, always planning toward Rennie's marriage. Tonight is the eve before the wedding day. It occurs to me that this small book will not be complete unless I tell the story of the wedding, the story which really began that day, long past, upon which I, a gay and heedless girl brimming with ready love, let my heart concentrate in a glance upon a tall slender young man intent upon his books, a studious reserved young man, in whom I divined a profound and faithful lover. I suppose, to be honest, that what I saw first in Gerald was a man so beautiful to look at that I was startled into love.

I said to Mary this evening when we were washing the supper dishes together and Rennie was smoking his pipe on the terrace, for he has taken on manly airs nowadays:

"Mary, my dear," I said, "I hope that Rennie will be a good lover and husband to you. I had such a good lover and husband in his father, and I hope the capacities are inherited, but I am not sure they are."

The tall lovely girl smiled her calm smile. "I am sure Rennie has inherited his father's graces," she said.

"I had sometimes just to suggest a thing or two to his father," I said.

"I will remember that, Mother," she said.

It was the first time she had called me "mother," and I was overcome with a new joy and stood, dish in one hand and towel in the other. She laughed then and put her arms around me and kissed the top of my head. She is that much taller than I. And I smelled the sweet scent of her bosom and was glad for my son's sake that she is a sweet-smelling woman, her breath as fresh as flowers without perfume.

. . . The wedding day has dawned mild and bright. We do not have hot days in June, not usually, and this one was cool and very clear. Early in the morning George Bowen drove up to the gate in a small gray convertible car, a vehicle old and dusty, and I saw him for the first time, a tall fair young man, with the same air of calm that Mary has. He stepped over the door of the car and sauntered into the house, his wrinkled leather bag in his hand, and he was as much at home as if he had come before. I liked him at first sight. He cuffed Rennie amiably, pulled his sister's ear affectionately, and spoke to me as though he loved me.

"I know you very well," he said. "I've wanted to meet you ever since I first saw Rennie."

"Put down your bag and sit down to breakfast with us, George," I said.

"I'll just wash my hands here at the kitchen sink," he said.

I liked the way he washed his hands, carefully and clean, as a surgeon does. George is a scientist, nuclear, one of the new young men. I had been a little afraid of him when Rennie talked about him. I saw a young man, brilliant, hard, perhaps unloving, as I suppose scientists must be nowadays. Instead here was this young man, kindly, affectionate, a fine friend for any lonely woman's son. Between these two for wife and brother, Rennie has his world to grow in.

"Eggs, George?" I asked.

"Please, fried on one side, thanks," he said, and folded his legs under the table in the breakfast alcove in the kitchen. I try not to be the sentimental motherly female we women are supposed to be, but I confess my heart was won when I saw how George Bowen enjoyed his food.

And all through this preliminary day he has made himself useful in a literal, practical sort of way. He persuaded the vacuum cleaner to work again, he carried chairs and cleaned the garage and was approved by Matt. And best of all was his tender understanding of Rennie and Mary. These two wanted no big wedding, and so about four o'clock in the afternoon they came into the house from wandering in the forest, and they went to their rooms to bathe and change to their wedding garments. Mrs. Matt was in the kitchen with a couple of neighbor women to help with the simple refreshments and she gave me a push.

"Get upstairs and dress yourself," she ordered me.

"It won't take fifteen minutes for that," I said.

"Then see if the bride don't need a pin or two," she said. "I remember very well myself that I needed a pin to the front of my corset cover, I was breathin' that hard."

I went upstairs then and when I had put on my pale-gray silk frock, I knocked on Mary's door and she called to me to come in and so I did. She was dressed and ready and was standing by the window, looking out over the hills. Her wedding gown was plain white organdy, embroidered at the hem and the neck with fine hand embroidery. She had made it herself, and it was exactly right for her. Around her neck was a little gold chain and a locket with Rennie's picture inside.

"Your bouquet is downstairs," I said. "Shall I fetch it now?"

The guests were already coming up the walk, and the minister was in the living room. In the morning we had cut flowers from the fields and put them into bouquets with delicate fronds of brake. But I had a few of my precious roses for Mary's bouquet. We cannot grow roses outdoors here in our cold valley, but I lift my rose bushes in the autumn and bring them into the cellar to sleep, where it is cool and dry and dark, and in the spring I set them out. This year I forced a half dozen to make roses for Mary. They are pale pink and pale yellow, and I cut six half-opened buds this morning and made them into a cluster and set their stems into ice water to keep them from opening too wide.

"Please, Mother," she said.

I went away at once for I heard Rennie leave his room. When I came back with the roses he was standing in front of her, holding her hands in his, and all my sorrow dropped away, never to come again. I am sure of it, for I know very well the look in my son's eyes as he stood looking at his bride. I saw it long ago in his father's eyes for me.

The wedding was perfect in simplicity. The valley people gathered in our living room, and all together there are only twenty or so for we invited no transient summer folk. When they were all there, Rennie and Mary, who had been moving among them, talking a little, smiling often, interchanged a look, radiant and tender. They clasped hands and went to the minister

and stood before him. Then without ado he rose from
his chair, and took his little book from his pocket and
spoke the few words that made them husband and
wife. We had no music, for among us only Mary has a
sweet singing voice. After the ceremony was over, the
guests surrounded the young bride and groom, and
I stood aside and wept quietly because they were so
beautiful, until Bruce Spaulden saw me and fetched
me a cup of fruit punch.

"Occupy yourself with this, my dear," he said, and
would not leave my side.

Mrs. Matt here set forth the wedding cake she had
made, a noble three-tiered confection, each layer different from the other. Mary cut the slices with Rennie's help, and they exchanged silver goblets, each
half full of the sweet wine I make every summer from
wild blackberries, while the guests enjoyed the sight
of them.

Then quietly, in the midst of the eating and drinking, the two went upstairs and changed to their trav-
eling clothes and came down again, and waving good-
bye they ran through the room, but waited for me at
the car. There my son swept me into his arms and
kissed my cheeks and Mary put her arms about us
both, and so I let them go. The guests waited to make
sure I was not lonely, and then one by one they went
away, and George Bowen was the very last, and he
stayed to put away chairs and carry dishes to Mrs.
Matt in the kitchen.

When he left he stooped to kiss my cheek.

"Good-bye," he said.

"Good-bye, dear George," I said, "and come back
often."

"I will," he said and then without the slightest sentimentality and as though he were declaring a fact, he said, "Shall I call you Mother, too, since now you are Mary's mother?"

"Do," I said gladly.

He winked his left eye at me. "Except you're too young to be a mother to three great gawks."

"Nonsense," I said.

He laughed and cantered down the front steps and stepped into his gray wreck of a car, without opening the door, and went off in a gust of smoke and gravel.

Now only Bruce was left and he stayed the evening with me. He knows that Rennie's father is dead. Rennie told him and then told me what he had done.

"How did you say it?" I asked, half-wishing he had not told.

"I said, My father is dead in Peking. My mother and I will never go back to China now. She will live here in the valley. But Mary and I cannot live here where there are no laboratories."

"A man must go where his work is," Bruce agreed.

"Well, your work is here," Rennie said bluntly, "and you must be my mother's friend."

"I want to be that and whatever more she will accept me for," Bruce said.

Telling me this a few days ago, Rennie looked straight into my eyes. "Mother, you will please me very much if you will decide to marry Bruce."

"Oh, Rennie, no," I whispered. "Don't—don't ask it."

"I don't ask it," he said. "I merely say that I shall be happy if you do."

To this I said nothing and perhaps I shall never say anything. I do not know. It is still too soon, and perhaps it will always be too soon.

It was comforting, nevertheless, to have Bruce spend

the evening with me, when everyone else was gone.
I lay on the long chair, and he sat near me, only the
small table between us, and he smoked his old briar
pipe and said nothing or very little. The silence was
comforting, too. I was very near telling him about
Gerald, and the house there in Peking, and all that
has happened to me. I thought of it while the evening
wind made gentle music in the pines and the mountains subsided into shadows. I thought of Rennie, too,
and of how he had been born, and this led me to Mei-
lan, whose child was being born perhaps upon this
very day. But in the end I said nothing and silence
remained sweeter than speech. When Bruce rose to
say good night, my life and love were still hidden
within me.

"Thank you, dear Bruce," I said. "You are my best
friend now."

He held my hand a long moment. "I'll let it go at
that, but only for the present," he said. He put my
hand to his cheek and I felt his flesh smooth-shaven
and cool. It was not hateful to me, and this surprised
me, too. But he said no more, and he went away.
After that I was suddenly very tired, but sweetly so
and without pain, and I went upstairs and to my bed.

. . . Days have passed again and I am already expecting Rennie and Mary to come home for the summer. I have had one more letter from Peking.

"It is my duty," Mei-lan insists, "to tell you that
I have borne a son. He is like his father. His skin is
white, his hair is dark but soft and fine. His frame is
large and strong. My mother says he will be tall. I
am astonished to have such a child. We two women,

180

my mother and I, we will devote ourselves to rear him well, for his father's sake and for yours."

Mine? Have I aught to do with her child? A strange question, and I do not know how to answer it. Then I remember that this child is Rennie's half-brother. It is possible that some day they will meet. How different will they be, these two? How much alike?

The ways of nature and of life are strange and deep. They are not to be understood. In the midst of angers and of wars love's secret work goes on, and binds us all by blood, and this, whether love is denied or love is bestowed.

. . . For you began it, Baba, you know you did. When the young pure American girl you loved would not love you enough to come to Peking for your sake, you flouted love, you said it did not matter and you took a woman whom you could not love. But she loved you, she bore your son, and one day I saw him and loved him utterly, and I went to Peking and made his city mine, until I was sent forth again, alone and forever parted from my love. Yet here are two grandsons, both yours, a globe between them, and still they are yours. And because they are yours, they belong together somehow, and they will know it some day.

What do you say to that, Baba? What do you say to that, old Baba, you lying up there alone on the mountain under the big pine tree?